Archer

Archer

DEBRA KAYN

New York   Boston

Copyright © 2013 by Debra Kayn
Excerpt from *Weston* copyright © 2013 by Debra Kayn
Cover design by Oceana Gottlieb
Cover copyright © 2013 by Hachette Book Group, Inc.

Forever Yours
Hachette Book Group
237 Park Avenue
New York, NY 10017
www.hachettebookgroup.com
www.twitter.com/foreverromance

First published as an ebook and as a print on demand edition: July 2013

Forever Yours is an imprint of Grand Central Publishing.
The Forever Yours name and logo are trademarks of Hachette Book Group, Inc.

The publisher is not responsible for websites (or their content) that are not owned by the publisher.

The Hachette Speakers Bureau provides a wide range of authors for speaking events. To find out more, go to www.hachettespeakersbureau.com or call (866) 376-6591.

ISBN 978-1-4555-7710-1 (ebook edition)
ISBN 978-1-4555-5092-0 (print on demand edition)

Wheels—I still think it's weird that we have more tools in our living room than we do furniture, but without your love of classic cars and motorcycles, the characters in the Hard Body series would've ended up with vehicles off the showroom floor. For that, I'm sure my readers thank you. Don't worry, I'll always go on a parts run for you and insist I'm too cool to change a tire. That's who we are, baby, and it's a good thing.

Gina—Girl, you're always there for me. You've calmed me down, made me laugh, and can throw my snippy back at me so hard, I have no doubt we were meant to be besties. Onward and upward, and we'll meet at the top.

Sasha H from Caribbean Accent Book Reviews—This one is for you. Your encouragement, fabulous attitude, and love for my books mean more than I can ever say.

Acknowledgments

To my editor, Latoya Smith, who made the Hard Body series a reality, I'll be forever thankful to you for teaching me the skill of toning down a super alpha hero without him losing his coolness factor. Thank you for seeing something special in my writing and being a fab-freaking-tastic editor!

Stephany Evans, my wonderful and patient agent and president of FinePoint Literary Management, thank you for all your hard work and dedication. I'm excited to have you by my side. Thanks for taking the stress off my shoulders, so I can concentrate on writing.

My super-awesome beta readers for this series, Tiss and Carin, who let me know early on that I had something wonderful with the Beaumont Body Shop boys and to stick with it. To hear the words "Is this going to be a series? I want MORE!" are the best motivating words an author can hear.

And last, but not least—'cause the Chicker Gang members should never take the backseat! Thank you to my street team for everything you do, the honest reviews, the motivation, the excitement, the questions, the hugs, the constant friendships, and for getting the word out about my books. I couldn't do this without you all. Go, Chickers!

Archer

Prologue

Mr. Anderson, Jane's employer, waved over his shoulder and wished her a good night as he pushed through the front doors of the attorney's office. She echoed her own good wishes and removed her purse out of the bottom drawer on her desk before the door stopped swinging. She thought he'd never leave.

Every minute past seven o'clock put her on edge. Scott hated when she came home late, no matter what day it was or how many messages she left on his voicemail informing him she was required to stay at work. She glanced at her watch. Maybe if she took the freeway instead of driving through downtown, her tardiness wouldn't raise Scott's suspicions.

The cool wind swept over her as she locked the door and stepped out from under the awning. She shivered, holding her keys in her hand and hurrying across the parking lot. Her red Duster, a Sweet Sixteen birthday present from her dad many years ago, parked at the end of the lot was the only remaining car left at the miniplex.

The bloodred paint with metallic flakes sparkled from the light of one of the security lamps dotting the area, filling her with warmth and a reminder of home. Her brother, Garrett, surprised her when she graduated college by painting her car and detailing it out. His friend Kage was responsible for the mag wheels that grabbed every man's attention who drove by. She raked her teeth over her bottom lip. Scott hated those wheels. He'd become enraged when he found out Kage gave her a gift that cost over a thousand dollars and split her lip when he slapped her.

At least she got to keep the tires.

Her car reminded her of everyone she loved. Her dad, Garrett, Kage, and her old friends back in Bay City, Oregon. She'd give anything to return home. Now even that dream was lost to her. Scott had proven he'd find her anywhere she tried to run.

Tension crept over her shoulders. The man seemed to find fault in everything she did lately. The male gas company employee looked at her funny, and she missed two days of work because Scott locked her in the house. The wrong number on her cell phone caused him to drag her along on business in the middle of the night because he claimed she was untrustworthy.

It was during those night errands that she learned the truth about the man she lived with, had thought she'd fallen in love with while in college. He was secure, attentive, and paid her more attention than any college-age guy she knew. If only she'd been smart enough to see past his lies before everything changed.

A car alarm blared somewhere in the distance. She picked up her pace, jogging across the lot. The last time she'd arrived home late, Scott threatened to make her quit her job. It was important that she follow his rules, because her job was the only thing keeping her from being entirely dependent on him. Someday, maybe she'd work up the courage to ask one of the two attorneys she worked for to help her get away from him.

It was getting harder to ignore the fact that all her suspicions were true. Scott Carson was the main supplier for the heroin in the area.

He also had a team of men who'd do anything he ordered, including killing her if she didn't drive him to do it himself.

There was no way he'd allow her to leave. She knew too much, and she was afraid his threats would come true. She wasn't ready to lie down and let him take her life.

An engine revved along the street, and she turned. The sight of the shiny metal emblem on the hood of the car as it turned into the parking lot paralyzed her with fear. Blinded from the headlights aimed at her and growing closer, her flight response kicked in and she sprinted the last thirty feet to her vehicle.

She plowed into the side of the Duster, scrambling around the front bumper to the driver's door. Adrenaline shaking her body, she grasped the handle and yanked. She muffled her scream and looked around on the ground. Somewhere in the lot, she'd dropped her keys.

She lifted her gaze, hoping she had enough time to run back, but it was too late. *Shit. Shit. Shit.*

Scott rolled out of the backseat of the Mercedes, followed by two of the many men he had at his disposal. She slipped her hand into her purse, pushing her wallet, sunglasses, and makeup bag to the side, searching for her cell phone. If she could push 911, maybe there was a chance she could stall him until help arrived.

"Do you know what time it is?" Scott approached her.

The short brown hair she used to love to comb her fingers through made his sharp nose look even more angled. She ran her thumb over the keypad, counting the buttons on her cell. At one time, she found him striking and regal looking.

A head taller than she, he'd looked down that nose at her too many times for her to find him handsome anymore. She swallowed hard, knowing whatever she said or how many times she tried to explain that when her boss asked her to stay late, she was going to be later than normal getting home.

"I'm sorry," she whispered.

Scott's hand shot out and grasped her neck, shoving her against the car. She dropped her purse and grabbed for his wrist, unable to breathe. Lifted off her feet, she kicked her legs trying to knock him off balance to take the excruciating pressure off her neck.

He pressed his lips against the side of her head. "What did I tell you I would do if you fuck around on me?"

She tried to shake her head, but his grip tightened. The outer corners of her vision darkened, and she struggled to draw air into her closed throat. Her gaze darted to the two men standing yards away, securing the area, and silently pleaded for their help.

They ignored her. She was only their boss's girlfriend, the troublemaker. She'd overheard Scott threaten to kill them on many occasions if they looked, spoke, or thought about her, and going by their reaction, she believed he'd do it too.

Welcoming the darkness that followed, she stopped struggling, because she knew she'd pass out at any second, and she'd be able to ignore what was happening to her. Pain shot up her knees and elbows, and the solid ground gave no cushion to her tender body. She blinked, rolling to her side. Scott's oxfords landed in front of her face, and she realized he'd dropped her to the asphalt in front of him. She coughed, gasping in air. Her throat burned and her whole body screamed from the abuse.

Scott's foot lifted. She squeezed her eyes closed, steeling herself. Blunt force knocked her sideways at the same time her breath escaped and a piercing pain shot through her midsection. She drew her knees to her chest to block any more kicks but wasn't fast enough. He stomped on her ribs, rolling her over under the force of his blow.

Scott squatted down, grabbing her hair, and shoved a pistol in her cheek. "Open your mouth, bitch. You know the rules. The only person you answer to is me."

She clamped her lips together and shook her head but grew light-headed and had to breathe. She gasped, sucking in air. Scott shoved the barrel of the gun into her opened mouth. She moaned as the steel clanked against her teeth. Hyperventilating, she stilled, afraid she'd finally pissed him off and he was going to kill her.

He'd threatened it many times over the last two years. At first, she talked him out of his anger, asking him to forgive her for whatever he imagined she did wrong. Then she'd retreated when the demands reached a level that was untenable. The most she could do was grovel and beg his forgiveness, promising she'd try harder.

"As of right now, you no longer have a job. You won't take a piss without asking me for permission first." Scott pulled back the cocking mechanism without removing the gun from her mouth. "And if you even *think* about telling anyone or asking one of those fucking attorneys for help, you're dead. Do you hear me?"

He jabbed the pistol in farther, knocking against her molars, causing her jaw to clamp down in reflex. She squeezed her eyes shut against the agony at the same time her upper body went in a different direction, and an intense piercing pain took the air from her lungs.

She mumbled around the gun, pleading for her life. Scott spit on her face. "Let's see how bad you want to live. If you make it home on your own, I won't kill you...this time. But if for some reason you don't show up in an hour, I'll make a phone call to one of my men who'll be following you. And then...well, you know what happens next, don't you?"

Then the gun was gone and someone tossed her keys on her chest. A few seconds later, a car engine roared to life and drove away, leaving her alone. She lay on the ground, unable to draw enough air into her lungs. Something was seriously wrong this time. She cried out as she moved her arm to feel her side, positive her hand would come away bloody. But there was no wound, only the worst pain she'd ever experienced.

She prayed for what seemed like hours, but no one came to her rescue. Her body soon shook from cold, which hurt but motivated her to try to get into her car. Hunched over, she held her ribs, sure that they were broken. It was impossible to inhale or exhale in more than short puffs. She clung to the side of her Duster to keep on her feet.

A police cruiser sped by with lights and sirens blaring. She slid into the driver's seat. Exhausted, aching everywhere, and light-headed, she sat there with her eyes closed. Scott had too much power and too many men working for him to think she could get away tonight.

He'd often bragged about having connections in the police force, to eliminate her places to run. She dug her fingers into her purse, pulling out the few receipts she'd folded perfectly and kept in the side pouch. Carefully, she unfolded them all until she found what she was looking for.

Hidden among the old grocery receipts was a small piece of paper with a phone number on it. Tears rolled down her cheeks unchecked as she folded her lifeline back up and hid it in her purse. She'd never found the courage to call, but having that piece of paper gave her hope that someday she wouldn't be living the life that she'd made for herself.

She wasn't stupid, no matter what Scott thought.

She had to get away, but that wasn't happening tonight. No, she'd wait until her ribs healed and she had enough strength to plan her escape better. This time she'd succeed.

She started the car and backed out of the parking spot. Once she made it home, she'd grow stronger and prepare for Scott to come after her again. If she had to kill him, then so be it.

Chapter One

Three months later

The three overhead garage doors at Beaumont Body Shop closed, and the remaining cars parked behind the building drove away. From the kitchen window, Jane Beaumont could see across the parking lot to her brother's shop. She dumped the water from her glass and set it in the sink. A longing to join Garrett and the men who worked at the shop—wherever they were going—bubbled to the surface, surprising her.

She'd remained hidden in the house during the day since returning home. Brushing her hair behind her shoulder, she thought about her life before Scott as she leaned against the counter. It was difficult to slip back into a life that no longer seemed familiar. She wasn't sure how her friends would react to the change in her now that she was no longer the overconfident girl they remembered.

Bluff, her ruffian gray cat she'd brought with her, rubbed against her ankles and meowed. She scooped the cat into her arms. "The boys are gone. We better go make ourselves useful, so we don't over-stay our welcome with Uncle Garrett."

Her phone rang. She shifted Bluff to her other side and pulled the cell out of her back pocket. *Please don't let it be him. Please don't let it be him.*

Jane was relieved to see the call was from Sabrina Wilcox, her best friend. She let it go to voicemail. Answering the call would mean she'd have to explain why she'd lied every time they talked on the phone. If she answered, Sabrina would figure out she was back in town, and she wasn't ready to talk about it yet. Not until it was safe.

Still carrying the cat, she walked into her bedroom, picked up her purse, then headed out the backdoor. Bluff meowed, wanting down. "Maybe next week I'll let you explore. You're not ready for the out-doors yet."

Used to being allowed to roam outside, Bluff sounded her dis-pleasure. Jane hurried the rest of the distance, slipping through the front door of the garage. She locked it behind her and set Bluff on the floor. Her heart raced, and she leaned against the door. Hating herself for worrying, she tried to act normal, completely aware of how crazy it was that she was doing this to please a cat.

"Fine, go explore." Bluff scampered off, then looked back at her and meowed before darting through the doorway into the shop. She squared her shoulders. It wasn't fair to keep Bluff inside with her, but she promised the cat she'd keep her safe.

The aroma of grease, metal, and paint lingered in the air. A famil-iar smell she grew up with, since her dad once owned the garage her brother, Garrett, now ran. She'd spent hours in here playing, bother-ing her father, and being a brat. She flipped on the hallway light and headed toward the office.

Garrett had no need for a daytime secretary. Most of the jobs that came through the garage were billed through the customer's insurance company or paid in full upon completion. The honor system on which her dad built the business worked well.

One hundred percent satisfaction guaranteed, and the boys from Beaumont Body Shop—her brother, Lance McCray, Tony Weston, and Kage Archer—were the best on the West Coast. Their awards, plastered all over the shop, were proof.

She unhooked the coveralls from the lockers lining the hallway. Doing laundry wasn't part of her job description, but since she was here, she might as well do it.

Kage's compartment had been left open, and she stopped. If she opened the other lockers, she'd find girly calendars, pictures of their polished cars, and half-eaten moldy sandwiches.

Not Kage. He had only one thing taped to the inside of his door. An old photo, curled at the edges, of a stretch of blacktop with a line going down the middle. She'd noticed it the other night, but no matter how many times she thought about it, she couldn't figure out its significance. She walked away and headed to the office.

Two steps into the cluttered space, she tossed the coveralls onto the chair and stopped. Her skin tingled. Something was wrong.

Why is the light on?

Garrett always shut everything off before he left. Without another thought, she dropped the bundle of clothes, whirled around, and ran. Before she made more than a few feet, someone grabbed her.

"No!" She fought, hitting a solid body. "I'm not going back! Please, don't make me go back!"

A male grunt propelled her into a panic. She reached behind her, blindly trying to pull hair. She kicked her feet, connecting with shins. Lifted higher, she slammed her head backward, unable to dislodge the strong arms circling her waist.

Her purse! She squirmed, trying to get her hand to her side. Her fingers curled around the cool metal of the pistol lying at the bottom between her hairbrush and makeup.

An arm came up and tightened across her chest, pinning her arms to her side. "Jane," he grunted. "Look at me."

She stilled, allowing her eyes to ease open as she recognized his voice.

"It's me," the man said.

She tilted her head toward him and looked into the gorgeous face of Kage Archer. His jaw hardened as he glared down at her. "Are you done fighting me?"

She nodded, letting the gun fall from her fingers and extracting her hand from her purse. "Let me down."

"Explain why you were fighting me." His hold remained tight, and his broad chest left her no wiggle room.

"You scared me. I thought I was alone." She jerked, but he wasn't letting go. "Have you ever heard of letting someone know you're in the room? You're worse than Garrett, always sneaking up on people and scaring them half to death. You should make a little noise when you walk."

He inhaled deeply. "My job is about *not* announcing my arrival."

Of course. All the guys who worked at the garage were private investigators who used the shop as their headquarters, preferring to detail and paint cars during their downtime.

"Now that we have that squared away, how about letting me go?" she said.

"Why do you come here at night instead of working during the day?"

"That's none of your business." She put all her strength into pulling away and felt his arms relax. He held onto her as her feet touched the ground again, letting her gain her balance. "Sheesh.

Maybe I like solitude, and not putting up with your overbearing attitude."

His face softened. "Janie..."

"It's Jane."

God, he was sexy. All the men who worked for her brother had reputations of being popular with the ladies. Seen together the four of them could cause an ovarian explosion. But Kage had it all.

Tall, broad shoulders, strong forearms, and a quiet presence, he was her ideal of the perfect man. His hair was the perfect shade of midnight. He kept it too long and looking like he'd crawled out of bed, raked his hands through it, and said *screw it*. It was a good look. A look she couldn't help watching out the window during the day when he was working, and she couldn't sleep.

A habit she tried to break, because the last thing she needed in her life was a crush, and certainly not on someone she'd watched while growing up and who had told her in no uncertain terms years ago that he wasn't interested in her.

Sexually numb the last eighteen months, she hated yet loved the way her stomach fluttered at the sight of him. Her heart raced, not out of fear but excitement, and her nipples constricted in pleasure.

She sat behind the desk, putting distance between herself and Kage. "Aren't the boys somewhere waiting for you?"

He continued to stare. She opened the drawer, nervous from the way he was looking at her. It was intense, and hot. It confused her. He should have no reason to be suspicious of why she'd come home. Garrett had promised to keep her secret.

Yet Kage looked at her the way any woman would want a man to pay attention. She glanced at him again. He was still staring.

Only four years younger than Kage, she had always reacted this way around him. Despite the fear Scott sparked in her, Kage was the only man she felt safe around or attracted to. She often wondered if he was the reason Scott forbade her to be around her family. Because when Kage was near, she had a hard time hiding her feelings. Even at the start of her relationship with Scott, when she was supposed to be madly in love, she couldn't help wanting to go home and visit because Kage always showed up to see her.

And yet she felt like they were running in opposite directions. He'd gone away to college when she started high school, and then she'd left to go to college when Garrett and his friends came home and decided to go into business together. After her dad retired, her brother and his partners kept the garage open—though even retired, they could never get Dad out of the garage.

During those years, she'd stayed away, because she was too ashamed of the life she had for herself. She thought she could handle Scott on her own. She thought she could get away. But Scott always caught her.

"Talk to me." Kage leaned against the desk.

She shuffled through the stack of papers. "There's nothing to say. I have work to do."

It'd take a month to explain her life. She'd fallen helplessly in love with Scott four years ago. At first, because she fell for his charm, she ignored the questions about where Scott got his money when he didn't seem to hold a normal job. His tongue was more silver than the necklace she wore around her neck. Later she kept her questions to herself, for fear of knowing the truth. Denial remained her best friend. Then, a year ago, everything changed. Her dad died of a heart attack. She made it back for the funeral, but Scott arrived the next day. She and Garrett argued. He'd wanted her to stay, but she wouldn't allow Scott to bring trouble down on her brother.

The funeral was the worst day of her life. She forced herself to walk away from the one place she felt safe. Her chest ached remembering. One man gave her courage to set her plan in action, and she'd never forget.

When she'd walked out to her car to leave, Kage had pulled her aside and handed her a slip of paper with his cell phone number on it. No words, no lecture; he just gave her the paper. She'd shoved it in her pocket without thanking him. She still had the paper hidden inside her wallet, wrapped in a receipt from the grocery store where no one would find it.

He'd never know how many times she'd pulled that piece of paper out and thought about calling. She *wanted* to call. God only knew she should have.

"If you'll excuse me, I have to get back to work." She squeezed his arm and stepped over to power on the computer before glancing at Kage again. "I'm serious, Kage. I appreciate your concern, but I'm fine."

"Have you eaten today?"

"Yeah." She leaned over, hiding behind her hair.

"What?"

"I don't know." She rubbed her forehead. "A tuna sandwich at lunch, I think. Why don't you go find Garrett and ask him if he's eaten? He didn't come in the house for lunch. Knowing him, he's probably out grabbing dinner now. You could join him…maybe he'll even foot the bill."

His gaze hardened. "I'm not talking about Garrett. I'm talking about you. I want to make sure you're taking care of yourself."

"I'm not hungry. You shouldn't worry so much. Now, really, Kage, I need to work and I work better in silence." She softened her voice. "We'll catch up later and—"

"Janie?" he growled out.

"Jane." She rolled her eyes. "I'm not sixteen anymore. Nobody has called me that name since—"

His eyes warmed. "For someone who isn't talking to me, you sure have a lot to say."

"Fine. Silence starts now." She pursed her lips.

"Good. It'll be a nice quiet dinner for both of us," he said. "Come on."

She grabbed the mouse and clicked, willing the stupid computer to hurry up and load. "I need to work."

"Bullshit." He closed the space between them. "Let's go. I'm buying you dinner and a drink."

She pushed her rolling chair away from the desk, backing away from him, but he kept coming. She slapped his hand. "No, you're not."

"*Yes*, I am." He widened his stance and pulled her out of the chair. "What's happened to you? You're not the Janie I remember."

She rolled her eyes, then shook her head when he gave her a satisfied grin at seeing her reaction to his bossiness. But the woman who once laughed, joked, and had a stubborn streak to the point of being infuriating was gone.

"I'm serious, Kage. I have orders to input and bills to pay." She planted her hands flat on his chest. His muscles hardened against her palms, and she curled her fingers before she caught herself reacting to him again and pushed. He didn't move, but his gaze heated. Uh-oh.

"Please." She let go of him, but he snapped his hands around her wrists and pulled her toward the door.

"How about we do that silence thing again, starting now?" He chuckled.

"I'm not going with you." She dragged her feet. It wasn't safe to go out in public when Scott could be out there looking for her. But it was apparent that when Kage wanted her to do something, she was going to do it. She gave it one more attempt at the front door. "I can't go with you. What about Bluff?"

"Who?" He stopped.

"M-my cat. Bluff." She lifted her shoulder. "She's in the garage. I can't leave her in there."

"You've got a cat?" He spoke low, humor in his voice.

"Yeah. Not that it's any of your business." She pulled one hand away from him, but he only slid his fingers between the fingers of her other hand and kept her at his side. "She stays in the house with me. She'll be scared all by herself."

He kicked the door closed, reached into his front pocket, and pulled out a key. "Well, she's got a night in the garage to explore. I'm sure she'll love it." He locked the door. "It's about time both of you started living the way you're meant to live."

She stalled at his car, a classic Mustang, black, with enough chrome to deplete her bank account. She changed tactics. She swung around and put her hands on his hard stomach.

He looked down. "Get in the fucking car, Jane."

She pushed him, which didn't make him move, but felt good nonetheless. Finally, she got in the car. "God, you are such a jerk."

He leaned over, extended her seat belt, and whispered in her ear. "You'll eat, you'll drink, and you'll enjoy yourself. Watch, you'll see."

His breath tickled her ear and caused an avalanche of warmth to fall low in her stomach. Her heart constricted. This was a weird feeling. One she'd had before with Scott and never experienced again, warning her that she needed to put a stop to whatever Kage had planned. Her judgment of men sucked.

"You can't talk to me that way," she muttered. "I don't have time to goof around with you. There's stuff in the office that needs to get done before tomorrow morning, and unlike you, I do my best work at night."

He grinned, a full-on show that she amused him. Jane snorted. How could she forget how stubborn he could be?

"I'm losing this argument, aren't I?" She leaned her head back on the seat and looked at him. She'd missed his bossy ways.

He grinned at her. "Yeah, you are."

No way was she ready to explore the feelings Kage created inside of her. She'd already lived through the embarrassment of his rejection when she'd tried to kiss him years ago. He relinquished her to friend-only status. But, despite being friends, going out to grab something to eat with him was the worst idea ever. It would only open the door to her being hurt again.

Kage drove through town, heading toward Corner Pocket. She stared out the window, trying to ignore the close confinement of the car, the heat she felt coming from him, and kicked herself for not fighting harder. She wanted to keep the ugliness in her life from touching anyone she cared about, including Kage.

Her reaction to him proved one thing. She was pathetic.

Kage reached across the space of their seats and squeezed her hand. "Everything is going to be okay."

She whipped her gaze toward him. Her head pounded. "What did you say?" she whispered. It dawned on her what going out to dinner meant. "That dumbass. Garrett told you, didn't he?"

"Yeah." He glanced at her. "We won't let anything happen to you."

She turned away, pain slashing through her. The last thing she'd wanted was anyone knowing what she'd lived through with Scott. Now Garrett and all the others knew how weak she'd become. Why would anyone want her after she let Scott use her as a punching bag?

"Please, can you take me home?" she whispered, struggling to hold back the tears.

His thumb caressed the back of her hand, and she became aware that she'd never let go of him and was in fact squeezing his fingers tight. The last time she latched on to someone, she'd lost four years of her life. It wasn't going to happen again.

She let go.

"Are you okay?" he asked softly.

She nodded but spoke the truth. "No."

Chapter Two

Jane was upset that Kage refused to take her home. Instead, he placed his hand over hers and continued driving to Corner Pocket, a local bar run by her friend Charlene.

She only wanted Kage to leave her alone until she could figure out how to handle the threat of Scott coming after her. She'd already created enough problems in her life. Involving more people would make the situation worse. Scott was unpredictable and dangerous. He also had a harsh, unfair attitude toward anyone she knew before him, including Kage.

As Kage pulled into the parking lot, Jane sank farther down in the seat. Garrett, Lance, and Tony's cars were parked right under the flashing neon sign. "Just great," she muttered.

It was unfair of him to bring her here when the bar was full of people. If they were alone, she'd try to defend her decision to keep the guys out of her business. She knew them too well to think they'd step down and let her handle Scott on her own. Because they were going to Corner Pocket, there was a good chance she'd run into others she knew, and they'd ask why she returned or about her failed relationship with Scott.

Most of her friends had warned her to take her relationship with Scott slower, but she'd refused to listen. She truly thought at the time she was falling in love. Scott talked a good game and promised her the world. Stupidly, she'd believed him.

Kage led her into the bar and straight to pool table 3 without saying a word. She held her chin high, refusing to cower. Her mistakes were her own, and she'd take responsibility for them.

Garrett stood in front of her, wearing a dark blue Henley, blue jeans, and black boots. His brown hair was swept back from his forehead. He resembled their dad with the worry lines forming between his brows and the stubborn tilt of his chin. Sometimes she found it too painful to look at him, because it brought up the hurt of not being able to see her father as much as she would've liked. Time that she'd never get back now that her dad had passed away.

She walked straight up to Garrett, pulled him a few feet away from the others, and glared. "You promised you wouldn't say anything."

"I'm not apologizing." Garrett lifted his mug of beer, drank long, and wiped his mouth off with the back of his hand. "I should've done something four years ago."

"I have no one to blame but myself," she whispered.

"Don't put that asshole's abuse on you. You're a victim, and you did the best you could do under the circumstances. I'm proud of you for coming home." Garrett's chin lowered to his chest and he leaned closer. "But letting the agency protect you is something I'm not going to argue with you about. We'll keep you safe. Kage wants—"

"Hey, Janie. Welcome home," Tony called.

She lifted her gaze, forcing a smile as all the boys who worked at the garage joined her and Garrett. "Thanks, guys. It's good to be back."

She could see the boys' mouths harden and blinked away the tears blurring her vision. This was exactly why she'd wanted Garrett to keep her secret. She didn't want them to see how weak she'd become and feel pity for her. Garrett's friends had always overprotected her growing up, and she hated putting them in the position of helping her get out of the mess she'd created.

Each one of them was scary in his own right. They'd kill or be killed protecting those they loved or were hired to protect. The guys were certified in weaponry and martial arts, and, if pushed into a corner, were street smart enough to kick ass without making a sound.

They were more than best friends, who'd grown up together playing baseball in the summer and hanging out at each other's houses. They were brothers. They trusted each other with their lives and weren't afraid to put their loyalty on the line.

When Garrett shifted his focus in college to criminal investigation while obtaining his auto body certifications to join their dad in business, he shared his idea of opening the agency and asked the other guys to join him. No one who knew them was surprised to hear of their plans.

They continued to train with the best to provide investigating services, bodyguard duty, and protection for others, standing up for those who didn't have the power to fight for themselves. She wouldn't allow them to go head to head with her ex-boyfriend. She couldn't live with herself if they got hurt because of her.

Despite how qualified the Beaumont Body Shop guys were, they were only four men. Scott had many men at his fingertips to call in to do his dirty work. Men with no loyalty or integrity. Scott's men would outnumber the Beaumont guys. She'd heard enough of the rumors and witnessed plenty of unspoken looks to understand that Scott thought he was untouchable. He'd kill anyone who got in his way.

That's why she never told Garrett what she stole from Scott when she ran. If the guys knew she was carrying something Scott wanted, something so big he'd kill everyone to get it back, they'd react drastically. As long as Scott needed her alive, she was saving all their lives.

She took a step toward her brother, but Kage tugged her back to his side, looping his arm around her waist. His hand landed on her hip and stayed. She caught her breath, leaning against him, wanting to leave but knowing she wouldn't because touching him calmed her soul. Garrett's eyes went to Kage, and a slow nod passed between the two men. The unspoken conversation confused her, and she didn't like not knowing what was going on in their heads.

Lance elbowed Tony, and their eyes landed on Kage too. She frowned.

"What's going on?" she asked.

"It's about time. That's all I'm saying," Lance muttered.

Lance leaned against the bar beside Garrett, black T-shirt stretched across his broad chest, black jeans, and black cowboy boots. It wasn't lost on her that his black goatee matched everything about him. Although Lance attracted a lot of women, he couldn't compare to Kage's size and quiet strength. Kage made her feel feminine and protected, yet he gave her strength.

She turned to Kage. "What's Lance talking about? Time for what?"

Kage shrugged, pulling her tighter against him. His hand low on her back forced her to place her own hand on his hard abdomen to keep her balance, but she didn't try to pull away. She stayed there because, at the moment, without him acting like an anchor, she might cry over how disconnected she felt from everyone and how long she'd been gone from home. She'd missed out on their lives—and that was the last thing she had wanted to do. Not getting any clues from the others, she looked at Tony for an answer.

But the most talkative of them all waved his hands in front of his chest and smiled, showing off the dimple in his left cheek. She inhaled deeply for the first time since stepping into the bar. Tony was her buddy, the one who always made her laugh. It was impossible to stay upset with his laid-back attitude. His blond, sun-streaked hair and tanned skin looked like he could've walked right off the beach carrying a surfboard, yet he wore a leather jacket and boots. Despite his calm disposition, she knew Tony's carefree demeanor could turn ugly. Years ago, she'd run to him for help when she saw a man beating a dog at one of the houses in town. She watched Tony return the favor, beating the dog's owner bloody. Kage was there too, holding her back from entering the fray and getting into trouble. Tony had saved the dog, assisted Jane in treating its wounds, and helped her find a new home for the poor thing.

"Whatever." She pushed against Kage, but he refused to let her go. "You all have fun with your man jokes at my expense. I can see nothing has changed around here."

The smiles disappeared. Lance stepped forward. Kage's body stiffened beside her, causing Lance to move back, hands up and grinning big. Before she could give any thought to what passed around the group, Kage picked her up and planted her butt on a bar stool.

"Kage!" She pushed off the counter and had swiveled halfway around when he stopped her. "Stop manhandling me."

Emotions played with her body and the signals misfired. Her nipples peaked, and she hated how her voice lacked any real conviction. Even his roughhousing turned her on.

"Then don't push me away." He leaned closer. "You're here to have a good time, get out of the house, and hang with your friends."

She squeezed her thighs together to banish the fluttery sensation his warm breath on her face caused and looked away from him. Geez, talk about bossy *and* hot. She looked over the group of men and curled her lip. Idiots. Not one of them had the decency to step up and tell Kage to back off or to come to her rescue.

Anyone else would think they were on their sixth drink the way they were smiling all stupid-like, staring at her and Kage, but she knew better. None of them drank more than three beers when they had to work in the morning. Tomorrow was Thursday, a workday.

"Stay put." Kage walked away.

Other women turned and watched him stroll across the bar. Jane wrinkled her nose, confused why he'd even want to bring her out with the boys. Obviously he could have any one of the ladies here, and they probably didn't have a whacked-out ex-boyfriend trying to come after them. Yet he'd assigned himself the duty of getting her out of the office, vowing to protect her, and she didn't know why. He'd rejected her previously, so it couldn't possibly be that he wanted to be with her or spend time with her.

For a moment, she wondered what it'd be like if it were only the two of them, and not her brother and the other guys out on the town. She sighed. Those kinds of thoughts had to stop.

Kage would never be interested in her. She was damaged goods, and he was too…too…God, he was hot.

"Janie Beaumont-y." A female singsong voice jerked her away from eyeing Kage's ass.

She turned, smiling. "Charlene."

Owner and bartender Charlene Turner bucked all stereotypes. A former burlesque dancer from Vegas, she'd ended up in Bay City, Oregon, opened Corner Pocket, and set about taking care of everyone. Including Jane, before she'd left for college.

Nothing had changed in her absence. Charlene was the one person Jane allowed to come and visit her at the house. She'd wanted to confide in the older woman, but in the end, she'd put on a happy face. Charlene wasn't fooled, though, because after she left, a stream of her old friends started calling her on the house phone to talk. No one ever asked, but she knew they were curious and concerned about her. The less they knew, the better. That way Scott couldn't use any of them to get to her.

"It's good to see you out of the house." Charlene leaned her elbows on the counter. Her dainty silver bracelets, of which she had at least seven on each arm, tinkled. "Which one of those fabulous boys can I thank for bringing you here tonight?"

"Kage," she said.

Charlene's boisterous laugh startled the patrons at the bar and proved Lycra really did keep voluptuous breasts contained in a low-cut top. Everything about her she did big. Her dyed red hair, which she teased, sprayed, and sprayed again to get the maximum volume, stood out, drawing much-wanted attention to her. Everyone knew she was happiest being center stage. Her attire of choice could still be used on the stage or a pole, despite her hitting the age of fifty-five. Nothing stopped Charlene from being who she wanted to be.

"I knew it. That boy's been chomping at the bit for years. Too much to handle for most women, but not you. I'm surprised it's taken him this long since you came back to do something about it," Charlene said.

Jane leaned forward. "What are you talking about?"

"Kage Archer, my girl." Charlene spotted him and whistled softly. "That man is an eight-cylinder engine purring under a beautiful, chrome-plated hood. A woman would have to buckle in to get a ride out of him."

"It's not like that." Jane sighed, shaking her head. "He's just doing Garrett a favor. You know how all of the boys are. I'm not the same person they knew before I left for college. I won't involve them in my life."

Charlene looked at her. "That's the stupidest thing I've heard. No one can help you, because you refuse to talk about what you're going through and think you can handle it yourself. You can't."

"I am."

"You are not." Charlene lowered her voice. "Besides, Kage isn't looking at you like you're Garrett's little sister. That man wants you, and he's tired of waiting."

"He does not w—"

"Look at you." Charlene straightened. "Wavy, full hair with natural ginger highlights women can't even pay their stylist to create, eyes the color of whiskey that intoxicate Kage whenever he looks at you, and boobs that I wish I had in my younger years. You have enough spirit inside of you to keep a man on his toes, and that's what every man wants. Kage's not immune to it."

"You're biased, because you're my friend," she said. "I'm trouble."

"I love you. Don't be talking down about yourself. Sure, you lost yourself for a while, but you're back. Kage knows it. He's always known it. That boy has had his eye on you before you even knew he was looking. I'll tell you, a man who's waited that long isn't going to sit around while you pull yourself out of the pond of self-pity you've thrown yourself in. Mark my words, Kage's marking his territory." Charlene lifted her brows and leaned closer. "Big-time."

Jane swallowed and stared across the room in disbelief. "No…"

"Yes, darling. That man wants you in his bed and in his life. He's not someone who changes his mind." Charlene laughed, squeezed Jane's hand, and then glided down the bar to help a customer.

It'd always been Kage for her. Even clear back when she wanted her first kiss to be with him. She'd planned, dreamed, and patiently waited until the timing was perfect. Or, so she thought.

She'd curled up on the couch with Kage when he crashed in the living room at her house after attending a bachelor party with her brother and had drunk too much to drive home. She'd been seventeen, trying to assert her newfound womanly feelings on the one man who made all those emotions explode inside of her.

He'd turned her down cold.

To add hurt to the humiliation she experienced, he'd kissed her forehead, turned her toward her bedroom, slapped her ass, and sent her away.

A deep hidden part of her wanted to jump up and go to Kage, ask him if everything Charlene said was true. But, having lived in hell the last four years, she knew she would only be setting herself up. No matter what Kage wanted, or she wanted, a relationship of any kind was out of the question.

Garrett and his friends wandered toward the pool table. As long as she could remember—even before they were of legal age—they'd gathered at table 3 and relaxed over a couple games of pool a few nights a week. She swiveled her stool to put her back toward the room. She'd eat and go home, hopefully with Garrett. From here on out, she'd be more careful and not let Kage catch her alone.

Just as the thought crossed her mind, Kage pressed his hand low on her back, sat beside her on the empty stool, and swung her around until she faced him, her legs inside his. "Whatever you're thinking, stop it."

She ducked her chin. "None of you were supposed to know. Garrett promised. I didn't want you to find out…"

He placed his hands on her thighs. "That was your first mistake. It's our job. You're our job, because we're friends. We all have a history together, and I care about you."

"I know," she whispered.

"We're experienced and trained to handle situations like the one you're in. Unfortunately, we deal with more women than we like who are in your exact position and need help."

"But you of all people know what could happen. Scott's not

working alone. He's not going to let me walk away. He might not come tonight or next week, but he'll eventually show up, because all I am is property to him. He's greedy and mean," she said. "I should never have come back here."

Her gaze lifted. His jaw ticked. She'd done everything wrong from day one. Going to college meant spreading her wings, and she not only flew, she'd gotten far away from who she was and then latched on to the first person who made her feel good about herself.

Kage tensed, letting his protectiveness show. She laid her hands on top of his. "There was nothing you could've done."

"I could've saved you," he muttered.

She smiled sadly. He had no idea how much she wanted to go back and do the right thing, to call him or Garrett the first time she suspected Scott was not a real estate broker but doing something illegal, but it was too late. "Let's not talk about it anymore."

"Okay. I'll leave it alone for now." Kage paused as the waitress brought two beers and set them on the counter. He watched her leave, then said, "From now on, you're with me twenty-four/seven."

"What?" She shook her head. "That's not necessary. I'm staying at the house, and—"

"I'm not going to argue with you. It's done." He picked up his mug. "Garrett's agreed."

"Oh, no, you are not staying with me." She tried to extract herself from between his legs, but he refused to let her go. "I can't be around you."

What he was telling her was impossible. Garrett could watch out for her. She worked at night. She'd stayed safe for the past three weeks. Scott hadn't called or found her. If Kage stayed with them at the house, she'd do something stupid.

"Really, Kage. You need to stay far, far away from me. For your own safety." She squeezed his hand. "Please."

His eyes went soft and he flashed a grin. Her stomach fluttered. She couldn't even sit beside him without melting.

"I'm serious." She raked her teeth over her bottom lip.

He kept looking at her in amusement, his smile growing bigger. "Me too."

Damn him. He wasn't taking her seriously. She was only entertaining him. "You'll see. I'll destroy everything."

"Baby, get this. I'm not telling you no this time. You got it?" he said.

Heat rushed to her cheeks as she remembered the last time he'd denied her. His gaze softened and she swallowed, overcome with the power and acceptance radiating off him. Her sex pulsed and dampened at what he was implying would happen between them if she let it.

"It'll never happen."

His gaze intensified. "It'll happen."

"I won't let it."

He hovered within an inch of her mouth. "It's already happened. Now you know. Deal with it."

"Never. Garrett won't let you stay after I talk to him. He's my brother. Family trumps best friends." She held on to the bar, pulled her legs out and over the top of Kage's, and jumped to the floor.

Moving before he could catch her, she hurried across the room and straight to Garrett. There was no way anyone was going to tell her how to live. She was done with that crap. She hadn't fought her way out of one situation only to end up in another one she didn't want or need.

Garrett leaned against the pool table, a pool stick in his hand, lining up a shot to the corner pocket. She grabbed a cue off the rack, pushed her way between her brother and the table, and held the stick in front of her, while she backed Garrett away from his game.

"Hey!" Garrett straightened. "What the hell are you doing, sis?"

Men at the other pool table moved forward. Several catcalls came over the noise from the bar. She ignored them all.

"Tell him." She pointed the stick across the room. Lance and Tony drew closer, grinning like two fools. She disregarded their amusement and concentrated on her brother. "Tell him he is not staying with us."

Garrett planted the end of his pool stick on the ground between his feet. "He's not."

Relief swept through her. At least her brother still had some common sense left in his head.

She sagged in relief, letting Garrett take the pool cue from her. "Good. I knew you wouldn't allow him to push—"

"You're staying at his house," Garrett said, tossing the stick to Tony.

Her heart skipped a beat and she recoiled. "What?"

Garrett moved around her and lined up his shot. "We decided the safest place for you to be is away from our house. Scott knows where to look for you, and he doesn't know where Kage lives. You'll be safer there. He's the best and he can protect you, sis. You know that."

"No…" She shook her head, unable to stop her hands from shaking.

Garrett looked up from the table at her. "Do it for Kage, sis. It was either let him take care of you or kill Scott."

She squeezed her eyes closed and swallowed hard before looking across the room. Kage sat watching her, intense and ready to pounce.

Garrett moved close. "He's hurting. You should've seen him, sis. He went crazy when I told him, and you know he never loses control. Let him take care of you. Let him do what he needs to do to keep you safe."

"I'll only hurt him more. I'm no good for him. My association with Scott is going to drag Kage down. You know he's sworn to stay far away from any kind of trouble, and you're just asking for Scott to walk right up to his door and knock. We both know if that happens, he will answer," she whispered, without taking her gaze away from Kage.

"Kage has his reasons." Garrett lowered his voice. "It's a done deal. You'll stay with him until this business with Carson is over, and we know you're safe."

She didn't know how long she stood there, but when Kage lifted his chin and mouthed *Come here* and pointed at the food he'd ordered for her, she returned to his side. She'd never let anyone she loved get hurt on account of her. She rubbed her hands over her hips, nervous about staying with him. Around Kage, she became distracted, and she couldn't lose sight of why she'd come home.

Chapter Three

Kage unlocked the front door of his house, took Jane inside, set the alarm, and flipped on the light. He did all that without letting go of her hand. He still had to keep checking himself, so he wouldn't move too fast. He didn't want to rush her after everything she'd been through.

He'd waited for the moment Janie walked back into his life, and now she was here. Years ago, it almost killed him to turn down her offer, her tempting lips, her innocence He squeezed her hand. She wasn't going anywhere.

He was in a better place in his life, no longer under the control of his uncle and stable enough to keep her protected from anything that could happen. He'd worked hard to make sure no one ever questioned his loyalty, his word, his integrity. He came from people who made running drugs their life. He was not one of them.

His biggest regret was rejecting Janie. He'd done it because he was unfortunate enough to have the last name of Archer and the stigma that came along with being connected to the underground. He'd taken those years without her to grow stronger, more determined, more stubborn for the day he'd prove his worth to her. Now he finally had the chance and he wasn't letting her go, no matter how much she wanted to deny she was still attracted to him.

The simple thought of her hurting or her being hurt enraged him.

Earlier, he'd wanted to go after Scott Carson. No one, especially someone who had one foot on the other side of the law and abused women, deserved to breathe the same air as Jane. If he'd known the kind of shit she was living through, he could've done something about her situation. Then she'd be in his bed, and Scott would be in a cold grave.

Jane's cat walked into the entryway and she gasped, tugging her hand from Kage's. He let her go and watched her swipe the cat off the floor and into her arms.

Bluff meowed a long string of cat words. Kage shook his head. It had seemed silly to ask Tony to leave the bar early to pick up Jane's things from the house, including catching the cat from the shop, but seeing her smile made him happy.

Always sexier than hell, she was even more beautiful than the last time he saw her at her dad's funeral. She wore her cinnamon-colored hair to the middle of her back, leaving it loose and tousled. Her high cheekbones gave her an air of sophistication to a perfect heart-shaped face. When she laughed, her lips curved up on the corners naturally, putting everyone she met at ease.

Despite her beauty, he couldn't ignore the way her self-confidence had taken a hit. He noticed her reluctance to talk, and at the bar she kept herself from looking at the others in the room. His Janie had always been the life of the party. She loved being the center of attention.

How a man could take someone full of life, with more spirit in her than the average woman, and try to stomp the goodness out of her was beyond him. What Carson did was a crime, and he'd pay.

All evening, Kage had stared into her eyes, wanting to find something that would convince him what he felt for her was all in his head. His fascination and attraction overwhelmed him at times, but one look from her, and he knew she was feeling their connection too.

"How did you get here? Hm?" she cooed to the cat.

Kage cleared his throat. "Tony brought him over for you."

She hugged the cat under her chin and glanced at Kage. Her beautiful brown eyes were leery, so unlike the amused, warm gaze he was used to. "I'm still mad at you, but thanks for letting me have Bluff."

"You'll get over your anger." He scooped the cat from her, dropped her to the floor, and pulled Jane before him. "We need to talk."

"About how you're going to take me back home?" She glared at him and flipped her hair over her shoulder, getting her bangs out of her face. "Or how you're going to stop touching me, because honestly, Kage, you're starting to—"

"No." He cupped her face and held her still. "You don't step out of this house unless I'm with you. If I'm busy, you call Garrett. If Garrett can't be here, call Tony or Lance. That's it. I don't care if Charlene or one of your girlfriends comes by to see you, but you can't go off with another woman without one of us guys with you."

"Kage—"

"This is not up for debate," he said. "I want to protect you."

"Scott hasn't even called. Maybe this time I'm really free from him," she whispered, searching Kage's eyes for confirmation.

"Then you'd be lying to yourself." He brushed his thumb over her cheek. "You've had phone calls at your house the last three days."

"What?" She covered her mouth.

"Garrett redirected the phone line to the shop during the day when you're not working and is fielding all incoming calls." Kage glanced away. "Scott doesn't stay on the line long enough for us to trace the call and find out his location, but the messages are clear."

She lowered her hand. "What does he say?"

"He's threatening you. Nothing specific, but his intent is clear. He always ends the message letting you know he's coming for you."

"I knew he would," she whispered. "I just wanted more time. I'm not ready to confront him."

"And you won't have to if you listen to me. Scott is growing impatient, and that kind of man is dangerous. I don't want you anywhere near him when he shows up," Kage said. "I swear to you, I'll get the asshole. He won't hurt you again."

"Maybe he'll give up and drop the idea that I'm his now that he knows I'm not alone," she whispered.

Kage wanted to do it, give her the security of knowing that that asshole was out of her life, but that'd be playing roulette with her safety. "He's definitely out there. I called in a few favors. From what I've heard of his recent actions, he's not giving up easily, or anytime soon."

"Favors?" She grabbed his wrists. "You haven't gone back to your uncle, have you?"

"No, but I will do whatever I need to keep you safe. That's a promise." Kage lowered his voice. "Garrett told me the story you gave him, but I need the truth. Every bit of it."

She pulled away. He let her go but followed her into the living room. The Janie he remembered never took shit from anyone. The Janie who stayed cooped in her house, worked nights by herself, and wasn't causing trouble for all the people around town was hiding something big.

The woman he knew before she shacked up with that asshole was still inside her. He saw the fire he remembered when she went head to head with her brother. Hell, every man in the bar noticed. Then a curtain fell across her face, and she retreated. He wanted his Janie back.

He turned on the lamp beside the couch. She paced the floor. He sat down, ready to wait it out.

"If you don't want your brother to know everything, it won't leave this room. I'll only give him the details necessary to help with the case." He watched her hesitate before continuing her walk. "I need to know."

She stopped. "Why?"

"Because…" He ran his hands down the thigh of his jeans. "I want to know what I'm working against and what I need to do to shut him down. I need to know how I can bring back the real Janie, not the one who's pacing in my living room, afraid every time I touch her."

She shook her head. "There's nothing you can do. Nothing anyone can do. He's untouchable."

"Come here." He patted his leg.

She crossed her arms. "No."

"Jane."

She lifted her chin. "Absolutely not."

"I'm not giving you a choice, baby. Get over here." He waited ten seconds, stood, and picked her up.

She wrapped her arms around his neck despite her previous protests. He took two steps before her body curved against his, and she put her head on his shoulder. His chest warmed, and a possessive urge to never let her go swept through him. He was doing the right thing.

He wanted to protect her, but he also had to be gentle, given her past. He had no idea what that bastard had put her through, but he knew Janie. Her reaction to him couldn't lie. She needed him, and he'd be here for her. However long it took for her to realize what they had together.

Instead of taking her to the couch, he carried her to his bedroom. At the foot of the bed, he stood her on her feet and reached for the waist of her jeans.

She slapped his hands away. "What are you doing?"

"You don't want to talk now, so we'll wait for the morning." He unzipped her jeans. "Now we go to sleep."

"Kage!" She stepped back, bumped into the mattress, and landed on her back on top of the bed. "God, this can't be happening."

He grinned down at her, pulled his shirt over his head, and tossed it to the side. "If we're not talking, we're going to bed."

She scrambled into a sitting position. "Fine. I'll go—"

He laid his finger on her lips, stopping the argument. She blinked up at him, and in that moment he saw the complete trust she'd given him. The look that kept him on the right path, aiming for the prize of being worthy of her if he stayed true to himself.

She wasn't scared or running away from what was happening between them. She simply waited for him to make the first move. He swept his thumb across her lower lip. Her mouth opened naturally, accepting his touch. His balls ached to take her right to the mattress and settle himself between her legs, but he was going to do right by her if it killed him.

"You're not going anywhere. I want you in my bed. We both need our rest, okay?" He stepped back, bent at the waist, and began unlacing his boots. "Your bags are in the corner. You can have the bathroom first. I took a shower at the garage, so take as long as you need."

"I'm not sleeping with you. I'll stay in your spare bedroom." She stood.

"Can't. No bed." He pried off his boot with his toe. "Before you ask, you're not sleeping on the couch either."

She stared at him bug-eyed. Bluff walked into the room, rubbed against Kage's socks, and then leaped onto the bed. Kage straightened and chuckled. The cat circled the bedspread, happy to plop onto her side and lie down for a nap.

"Take notes." He motioned behind her. "Look at Bluff. *She* wants to sleep with me."

"I'm not sleeping with you. You had your chance, and you tossed it away." She marched past him, picked up her bag, and disappeared into the bathroom, slamming the door behind her. "And my toothbrush better be in here, or I'm going home," she yelled through the door.

He removed his phone from his jeans pocket as he walked barefooted out of the room. His phone downloaded his messages, while he shut off the lights throughout the house and took one more look around. His house was situated on two acres on the edge of town. Enough property to afford him some privacy, and easy to tell if someone approached the house and keep Jane safe.

His cell vibrated on his way down the hall, heading toward his bedroom. He stopped and read the screen. The police reports he asked for—he quickly scanned the documents. *Fuck.*

He pivoted and went back and double-checked all locks and windows. He even reset the alarm by the front door that secured the entrances to make sure it operated perfectly. There was no room for mistakes.

Once he was satisfied he'd done everything he could, he returned to the bedroom, not surprised to find Jane still shut inside the bathroom. He flipped off the light, stripped out of his jeans, leaving on his boxers, and climbed into bed. Prepared to wait her out, he lay on his back, hands clasped behind his head.

The police reports burned inside his mind. She hadn't told Garrett the truth.

The door clicked, and Bluff meowed beside him. He picked the cat up and set her on his stomach, stroking her long fur.

A few moments later, the mattress dipped, and Jane lay down wordlessly, staying to the edge of her side of the bed. He exhaled quietly, relieved that she was over her snit and had stopped trying to fight him at every turn.

He set the cat beside him on the bed, rolled toward Jane, and wrapped his arm around her waist, pulling her back against his front. "Shh, I just want to hold you. I'd never do anything to hurt you."

Rigid and barely breathing, Jane remained quiet. It took at least a half hour for her body to relax.

His fingers sprawled on her stomach. "Janie?"

"Hm?"

"Do you remember what happened to my dad after my mom overdosed?" He inhaled the citrus aroma from her hair before kissing the back of her head.

She half turned, and he could feel her gaze on him in the dark. "Yeah."

Brent Archer was spending the last five years of a twenty-year sentence in the state penitentiary. Not only had his father been caught selling a large amount of heroin, he was linked to two deaths caused by the cut of drugs he sold to others.

His father's brother, Darrell, a well-known drug lord, took off for California afterward, scot-free, taking his drug runners with him. Kage inhaled deeply. Everyone in town knew his past, and he'd fought hard to prove he was nothing like his only living relatives.

The desire to prove everyone wrong, that he would not end up in prison or deal dope out of dark corners, drove him to keep to himself. He wanted no speculations, no angry ex-girlfriends, no scandal wrapped around his name. He'd set the bar high and intended to keep it that way.

Every woman he'd ever slept with or took out on a date never lived up to the one person he wanted and couldn't have. The other women lacked a quality he always held out for and never found. It wasn't hard to see the truth of what that something was when he was with Jane. Around her, he could be himself. She understood where he came from and accepted him no matter what.

There were never questions he avoided or fear in her eyes. She trusted him, respected him without asking anything in return. When his uncle came back a few years after his father was sent away, Jane and the guys still accepted Kage. Everyone else crossed the sidewalk if they saw him coming or looked at him as if he were dealing drugs right in front of them.

The doubts were always there.

Today, his uncle ran the biggest underground drug trade on the West Coast. But Kage was no longer a kid. After his father's incarceration, he'd gone to live with the Dentons, the local bank owner and his wife, who took foster kids in on occasion. They raised him from the age of twelve until he was eighteen. An older couple when they took him into their home, they both had died over the last four years, after living good lives. Without their intervention and support, who knew how he would've turned out?

He laid his hand on Jane's stomach.

"Kage…" She covered his hand with hers. "We don't need to talk about this."

He swallowed. "I want you to know, if it comes down to it, I'll contact my uncle. If we need him to get rid of Scott, I *will* call him."

Darrell Archer had enough power and wealth to get things done without a trace. No one would have to know Kage had been involved. He wasn't taking any chances where Jane was concerned.

"You can't." She pushed up and moved a stray hair from over his eyes. "I know what that would do to you."

He blew out his breath. "I've read the police reports."

She turned away from him. "God, Kage, don't tell my brother. Please don't tell him. He's been through so much with Dad, and—"

"Tell me. Tell me it wasn't as bad as it sounded in the report. That he didn't break your fucking ribs and shove a pistol in your mouth." She eased up into a sitting position. "Tell me that motherfucker didn't do something else that you left out of the police report."

"Drop it, please," she whispered.

"I can't do that, baby." His chest tightened. "Let me know what we're up against. Did he hurt you any other time?"

She eventually nodded. He squeezed his eyes closed before he answered. "How long did this go on?"

"The last year and a half. Before that, he just made sure he knew whatever I was doing. He had his goons watching me all the time. I was careful. I did everything right, so he wouldn't get upset." Her head turned. "I did everything right," she whispered.

"You did good, baby. You survived," he said.

"Did I? Because right now, knowing you found out what I allowed him to do to me feels a lot like I died the moment I left home to go live with Scott. I never wanted anyone to know, especially you. I knew how much you hated your family for what they put you through. I was afraid you'd hate—"

"Shh." He laid his chin on the top of her head and hugged her tight. "Never. You're here now. Nothing else is going to happen to you."

She trembled. "I'm afraid."

"No one will ever lay a hand on you again. I promise," he said.

She shook her head. "I'm not scared for me but for you. For Garrett. For anyone who stands in Scott's way when he comes for me.

And he will come. He always does. But this time I'm not going back."

He knew when he'd first read the statement, something was missing. He couldn't believe she'd endured this kind of pain for so long. Rage swept through him. He'd heard enough.

He lay his head down on the pillow beside her, keeping his arm around her. "Sleep now. We'll go forward tomorrow."

A few minutes later, she latched her fingers over his hand. "Kage?"

"Yeah?"

"What's going on between us?"

"Exactly what you think is happening," he said. "I want you. You want me. I will have you…but not tonight. When it happens, I'll have my Janie back. But I need you to come to me on your own. I won't rush you, but know once you do come to me, there will be no turning back."

She didn't say anything else, and it took her body a long time to relax. It was much later when he could tell she'd finally fallen asleep. Not long afterward, Jane whined in her slumber. He held her tighter, smoothing her hair back from her face. He pressed his lips to her skin, wishing he could erase the pain of what she'd gone through. If only he'd known the truth of what Scott was capable of or suspected the terror she was facing alone. He would've put a stop to her abuse and killed the bastard before he could lay another hand on her.

Bluff climbed up on the curve of her hip, and he lazily rubbed the cat between the ears and listened to her purr. He stayed awake most of the night, wishing they were together for a different reason, while imagining the many ways to kill Scott Carson.

Chapter Four

The last page slid through the fax machine as the phone rang. She glanced over her shoulder, waiting for the document to finish. Most of the shop's calls came through on the other line, for Lance concerning agency business.

She had no idea how busy the private investigating part of Beaumont Body Shop had grown. Garrett kept his client's jobs secret from her. She only knew enough to have some idea what his days and nights were like or where he was going to be on a certain job. She'd gained a new respect for the boys, but it also had led to more worry on her part.

She'd seen each of them leave at odd hours and couldn't miss the pistol strapped under a coat or tucked in at the back of their waists, a serious, almost fierce expression on their faces. Their job was dangerous, and they took it seriously.

At those times, she preferred to practice denial that they were putting their lives on the line. She returned to the desk. The phone rang again. Line 6 meant she needed to answer, because it was usually customers with accounting questions or wanting to bring in a job for the garage.

She clicked on the speaker. "Beaumont Body Shop, how can I help you?"

"You done for the day?" Kage obviously didn't believe in saying hey when he called.

"Why?" She shut off the computer.

"Yes or no?"

She shook her head, not ready to face going home with him. When she was working and alone, she had a firmer grip on her life. Around him, she seemed to forget what she was here to do—learn to survive on her own. Even though she'd slept better the last three nights in bed with him than she had in the last several years, she still wanted to be able to depend on herself.

"Maybe." She grinned, continuing the banter of teasing him into a better mood. He'd gone deathly quiet after his meeting with the boys this morning, and it'd taken her three trips into the garage afterward to bring him out of his stoic mood.

He chuckled. "When you're through, meet me in the weight room."

"I don't do weights." She laughed. "I have to check on Bluff and I want to do a load of wash. I'll go see if Garrett can drive me back to your house...unless you want to bring Bluff back to me and let me sleep in my own bed, which is much more comfortable than yours and has a big fluffy comforter."

"It's pink and has ladybugs," he said.

"Big whoop." She scrunched her nose, swearing she'd buy a new bedspread to replace the one she had since junior high. "Bluff likes it."

"Bluff likes sleeping on my chest."

That was true. Earlier this morning before the alarm went off, she'd lain there looking at Kage. She'd pretended to sleep, because it was comfortable curled against him with her head on his shoulder. She warmed. She also hadn't missed Bluff curled in her own cozy spot on Kage's bare skin. Or how Kage's hand lay on Bluff's back, periodically rubbing her fur throughout the night.

"Yeah, you're not so badass scary when you're cuddling a kitty, Archer." She smiled.

"I don't cuddle." She heard the laughter in his voice. "Five minutes. Weight room."

He disconnected the call. She shook her head. Obviously saying goodbye before hanging up was a waste of his time as well.

She pushed the speaker button off. The phone rang again, same line, and she picked the handset up this time. "Give me a break, Kage. It's been ten seconds."

"Thought you could outsmart me by taking me all across the fucking United States chasing you down? You thought wrong, bitch," Scott said.

Her heart raced and she couldn't move. "I left you, Scott. Leave me alone and move on."

"It'll never be over between us." His voice rose. "You're mine. You won't exist without—"

She slammed the phone down as her brother rushed into the room, skidding to a stop. She stared at him, wide-eyed, hoping he'd tell her it was a prank call and that was not her ex-boyfriend threatening her.

Garrett reached for her. "Next time keep him on the line as long as you can."

She'd expected Scott to contact her. Not one day went by that the fear of him coming to get her wasn't a real threat. Her body tingled, and her breath came too quickly. It had been three weeks without any sign of him contacting, except on the other line. She'd hoped he'd given up.

"What happens now?" She clung to his shirt.

"One step at a time. We let him make a move or get reckless. Whatever he decides to do, we'll be one step ahead of him. I won't let anything happen to you. I promise." He stroked her back. "You okay?"

She nodded. "He knows where I am now. He'll come for me."

"That's why we wanted you working during the day, while we're here." Garrett kissed her forehead. "Nothing is going to happen to you. You have to trust me."

She leaned against the desk. Her legs trembled, and she stared at the floor. She'd been down this road before. Her plans never worked out the way she expected. "I don't want him to come."

"I know you don't, sis. But this has got to end."

She hung her head. "I doubt if he'll be alone."

"I know that too."

"I need to get out of here." She grabbed her purse out of the desk. "I want to go home. I'll go to Kage's. Anywhere. I just need to get out of here before he shows up."

"Okay. Kage will take you home. He's in the weight room. I'll walk you there." Garrett put his arm around her. "It'll be all right, sis. We've got your back."

"Nothing about this is all right. It's especially wrong, because it now involves you, Kage, and the others. I wish I never came—"

"Will you knock it off?" Garrett held her shoulders and peered down at her. "What is wrong with you? I'm the first person you should run to when you need help. Instead, you've been trying to handle everything yourself, so tell me…what's wrong with me that you couldn't trust your own brother to keep you safe?"

She shook her head. "I do trust you. I just don't trust Scott."

"Shit," he muttered. "That attitude is going to stop right now. He has no power over you."

But, as she knew better than anyone, Scott *still* controlled her. No one could see how much was at stake. If Scott came and threatened all the people she loved, she'd go with him in a heartbeat to keep them safe. Scott wanted her and would do anything to get her. The thought scared her to death. Deep in her soul, she knew Kage, Garrett, Lance, and Tony would not let him touch her, but that didn't mean nothing bad would happen. She couldn't chance losing another person in her life.

Garrett walked her down the hallway, through the door into the extension he'd added last year to handle agency business. He'd given her the quick tour when she'd arrived home, but she hadn't set foot in this part of the building since.

Each of the boys had his own office, along with a lunchroom slash conference area, a weight room, and a fancy bathroom that beat the one-stall, unisex washroom used in the body and paint area. The control room, which looked like a smaller version of what she imagined NASA had, and two holding rooms completed the area.

For the first time, it dawned on her that investigations were their main business. She looked at Garrett. "Why do you continue to keep working on cars if this is what you love to do?"

Garrett paused outside the weight room. "It relaxes me. After a stressful day, there's nothing like zoning out spray-painting a panel or hammering the wrinkles out of a bent-up fender." His smile fell. "And all of this is part of who Dad was. I don't want to lose him."

She understood, more than he probably realized. She kept the memories of her dad alive in her head. She wasn't strong enough to deal with his loss.

As Garrett led her into the weight room, Jane couldn't help staring. No, what she did was ogle.

Kage hung upside down on a bench, his feet secured under a padded bar, doing sit-ups. Light-headed at the bulked-and-beautiful sight of him, she could only focus on the ripple of his abs.

Garrett chuckled. "I'm out of here. See you tomorrow."

"Yeah, okay…" She nodded, not taking her gaze off Kage.

"Stick with him, sis." Garrett kissed the side of her head before crossing the room to talk quietly with Kage and then leaving.

Kage detached himself from the apparatus, performing a neat flip to land on his feet. He snatched a towel off a nearby weight bench and wiped his face, draping the cloth around his neck. She gulped as he approached. The air seemed to disappear and her head got fuzzy.

He frowned. "You okay? You're not looking so well."

Of course she didn't. Her ex-boyfriend's phone call had freaked her out. Eight hours behind a desk, shut in a room with no windows, and the first beautiful thing she sees today was Kage in a pair of loose-fitting shorts, hanging off his hips, covered in sweat. Of course she looked rattled.

Any woman would find herself entranced and drooling. She lifted her hand to her mouth. Her fingers came away dry. *Oh, thank God.*

"You're the shit." The moment her opinion slipped through her lips, she wanted to take it back.

He smiled. Not a half grin, but an all-white-teeth spectacular aimed at her. A rock-her-world kind of smile. She groaned. No wonder he worked out; he had to carry around his big ego.

"Yeah?" He moved in closer, now wearing his teasing face.

"Oh yeah, totally hot," she whispered.

She could handle his angry face, even his scary face, but when he let it all fall away and acted like he did before her life had taken a downturn, he made her remember how she used to feel before Scott. She flinched and stepped away. "So, are you ready to go? I'm ready. We can go to your house."

His face got serious. "Are you sure you're all right?"

"I'm fine. Let's go." She turned around, because one more glimpse at his glistening body would send her into a full-blown panic.

He'd told her the next move was on her. If she wanted him, she'd have to show him. Right now, she could show him that and more.

"Let me grab a quick shower." He turned and deliberately held her gaze. "That phone call is a good thing. It might not seem like it, but the more we know, the better we can work this guy."

How could they all believe drawing Scott closer to her would be beneficial? The object was to stay far away from him. She wasn't going back. Scott needed time to understand she was serious.

"Come on, I'll take you to Lance while I wash up." He motioned for her to follow him out.

"I'll stay in here and wait." She needed time to calm down, and she couldn't do that with one of the guys always around.

"Not happening." He shook his head. "You can't be alone right now. The phone call from Carson is proof of that. Without a trace on the call, we have no idea how close he is. He could be anywhere. You're safe inside this building, but I want you used to having someone around constantly."

"I get it, but I'm already protected here," she said.

"You are not protected without someone with you. I don't care if you're in the building. You're certainly not okay if I think you're about to faint and you're alone. If I'm not with you, someone else I trust will be."

She lifted her purse, dug inside, wrapped her fingers around the handle of the pistol, and pulled it out. "I can protect myself."

He took a step back. His hands went to his sides. "What the hell are you doing?"

She waved the gun in his direction. "I've done okay on my own, and I can take care of myself and Bluff. I've been doing it for the last three weeks. Even if Scott gets near me, I can use this."

"Jesus, woman." Kage reached out, pushed her hand to the side away from him, and locked down on her wrist, prying the pistol out of her grip with the other hand. "No guns."

"Give it back." She put her hand out. "It's mine."

He twirled the chamber, peered inside, and cussed under his breath as he removed all the bullets. "The safety wasn't even on. You could've shot yourself or me."

"W-what?" She shook her head, stepping away. "Kage, I wouldn't have shot you," she barely whispered. "I've shot a pistol before with Dad and Garrett."

"Pointing a gun at my chest isn't the way to show me that, baby." He inhaled deeply. "No guns. You hear me?"

She crossed her arms. To survive Scott, she needed that weapon. "I don't see what the big deal is. I've seen you carry a gun."

"That's different. I have a permit and I'm allowed to carry." He frowned. "How the hell did you get this?"

"Stole it from Scott," she mumbled.

He stepped back, letting her go. His hands went to his head and he clamped his lips shut. She glanced away, expecting him to blow.

"You can't keep this kind of information to yourself if we're going to help you get this guy." He shook his head. "I don't know whether to laugh, because that's something the old Janie would do, or worry about you."

"Sorry." She chewed the inside of her lip.

"We'll talk when we get home." He pointed toward the door. "Let's go find Lance."

She led the way. Her purse strap slid off her shoulder, a lot lighter than when the purse had held the gun. She glanced behind her at Kage when she reached the control room door. "Can I have it back?"

He shook his head, grinning his sexy half smile. "No guns."

She turned around, sighed, and pushed through the door. She was tired of everyone telling her what to do. Somehow, she'd have to find another gun. She'd be ready when Scott came for her.

Chapter Five

Garrett shut the door of his Barracuda and strode toward the porch of Kage's house. Kage walked down the two steps and met him in the driveway. A quick glance showed the pistol in Garrett's shoulder holster and the firm grip on his emotions over Jane's situation.

"Hey." Garrett stopped and looked toward the house. "I got your message. Janie okay?"

Kage nodded. "If marathon baking means she's handling everything okay, then yeah, she's hanging in there."

"Shit." Garrett rubbed the back of his neck. "I wish that bastard would hurry up and show his face. It's killing me to wait around and see Janie beating herself up. I had no fucking clue what he was doing to her, or I would've removed her from Scott's clutches and made sure he never raised a hand to anyone else again."

Scott Carson would come soon enough. Kage stared out across the land. He couldn't picture any man walking away from Jane and being happy about it. Add in the fact that Jane was a liability to Carson's freedom since she knew more about his drug dealing than she let Carson know about; it was only a matter of time before the bastard showed his face.

"We all watched her pull away from us and didn't do a damn thing about it," Kage said.

"You don't think that bothers me?" Garrett cussed. "I think about it every second of the day."

"Guilt lies on my shoulders too." Kage glanced at him. "I believed her when I asked at your dad's funeral if she was happy. I thought it was the emotions of the day that put the sadness in her eyes. I even gave her my number, hoping she'd get to Pullman and realize she wanted to come back to Bay City. I should've said more and told her I wanted her here."

Silence stretched between them. Garrett was the one friend who understood him. He couldn't count how many times they'd sat outside in the dark, drinking a beer, maybe sharing ten words apiece and being okay with each other's company. They survived without all the bullshit most people needed in their lives.

He gave the Beaumonts credit for their constant support and their willingness to let him hang out at their house for helping him achieve what he'd accomplished in his life. Even Pop, Garrett's dad, had spent time with him when he lived with his foster parents, directing him on the correct path in life, showing him skills in the garage, and giving him a purpose. Kage never talked about how much their closeness meant to him, but he had a feeling they knew.

He had Garrett's back, and Garrett had his. Their friendship went back to when he was six years old and met on the playground. From then on, it was him, Garrett, Lance, and Tony. None of the guys cared if he came to school and fell asleep at his desk because his mom was strung out and kept him up all night or his dad had runners knocking on the door at all hours.

When he was older, they never questioned him why they never hung out at his house. He glanced behind him at the ranch-style home that'd seen better days and a lot of bad news. Not much had changed. The place still needed paint, and the yard was overgrown.

He'd heard the talk in town. People wondered why he'd chosen to move back to the house where his mother died. It was good to remember where he came from. It reminded him of where he needed to continue heading in his life.

"What's your plan, Kage?" Garrett faced him.

Yeah, Garrett knew him too well without him even saying a word.

He crossed his arms over his chest. "We're hitting dead ends. All background checks have fallen off the radar. We can assume Carson's going by an alias, but so far Janie hasn't given us anything else to investigate. There's no record of him. He hasn't even had a fucking speeding ticket within the six states we've gone through, but that may be because his hired men clean his past for him."

Garrett stepped over and leaned against the quarter panel of his car. "We've got surveillance up at the garage, my house, and your house. Legally, we can't go any further. We're screwed until he comes out into the open. All we can do is wait."

Kage met his gaze. "We both know that's not true."

"*No!* You're not going there. We can handle it on our own." Garrett's fist came down on the hood. "Sister or not, I'm not willing to lose you in the process, and the moment you even contact your uncle, he'll use whatever he has available to bring you into the underground. We can wait. Janie's safe at the moment."

Kage shook his head. "At the moment, but what about tomorrow or next week? How long are you going to allow her to jump every time one of us comes into the room? She's in the house, making more food than we can eat in six months, pretending to have everything under control. But we both know she doesn't. She's broken, and I want her back."

Garrett ran his hands through his hair. "Hell…what am I supposed to do?"

"Back me up with Lance and Tony if I contact my uncle." Kage swallowed down the bile. "We've exhausted all other avenues, but Janie's told us that Carson is dealing drugs. Darrell would know exactly who he is and where I can find him."

Garrett turned around, planted his palms on the car, and hung his head. "He'll pull a marker on you. If he lets you walk away, you'll live the rest of your life wondering when he's going to call you and demand you repay him."

"Hell, I already do. You know that, man," he said.

What Garrett didn't know was that Kage wasn't powerless. If push came to shove, he had one card that trumped anything his uncle could do to him, and he was going to rely on that insurance. He'd held on to the one thing that'd save him from going into business with his uncle since he was twelve years old.

"Promise me you won't make contact without letting me know first." Garrett raised his gaze, and Kage recognized the same stubbornness set in his mouth as he saw on Jane when she grew angry. "Give me the chance to talk you out of ruining your life."

"It's for your sister," he said, reminding Garrett of why they were having this conversation.

He'd always refused to talk about his and Jane's relationship with Garrett, even though all the guys at the garage knew where he stood. He'd never acted on his feelings, and had kept Jane from ruining her life by setting her sights on him. But that was in the past. He'd sorted his life out and was ready to prove that he could take care of her.

"She's got feelings for you, you know." Garrett spoke softly. "I remember her throwing herself at you in high school. Hell, she still looks at you and loses herself."

"Yeah." He leaned against the car next to Garrett. "I do want you to know I'd never hurt her, and I'd kill anyone who harms one beautiful hair on her head."

"She's not ready to thrust herself into another relationship." Garrett spit on the ground.

Kage nodded. "I know that too, but you'll have to accept that there's no way the two of us can live together and not have something happen between us. We've skirted around each other for the last seven years. I'm not running anymore, and I'm not letting her get away this time."

"Fair enough." Garrett inhaled deeply. "Now you can listen to me. When your mom overdosed—"

"We're not talking about that." Kage pushed off the car and moved toward the house.

"You owe me if you think you're going in there and laying this on my sister's shoulders. She's not strong enough to deal with Carson *and* you," Garrett said.

Through the years, Garrett had pushed Kage only twice to talk about what happened the night his mom died with a needle in her arm, the night his dad went to prison and his uncle escaped the Bay City area, leaving him all alone with a bad reputation. Both times he'd walked away.

He stopped but refused to turn around.

"If you have plans to seek vengeance, you'll not only lose your spot at the agency, but I'll walk away from our friendship and make sure Janie never has anything to do with you. She deserves better," Garrett said. "You can fool everyone that you've moved on from the shit storm your family passed down to you, and most days I believe you have. But there are times like tonight and the other day when I broke the news about why Janie came home that I see what you're capable of, and it makes me wonder how well I really know you."

Kage's knees buckled and he turned, widening his stance to hide how much Garrett's words affected him. He wanted to deny everything his friend said, but Garrett expressed the fear he lived with every day when he woke up. Would today be the day he walked across the line?

"I think you're strong enough to prove me wrong," Garrett said. "I fucking hope you prove it to Janie. You're the man she's loved all these years."

Kage lifted his chin, acknowledging that he heard Garrett loud and clear. Garrett looked at the house, and Kage waited for him to change his mind. He'd done everything in his power to earn Garrett's trust, but Jane was his sister, and he understood why Garrett would protect her. They were the only family each other had left, and their bond was strong.

Garrett moved to the driver's door, knocked on the top of the car twice in a sign he was done talking, and slipped inside. Kage watched him back out of the driveway and roar off, leaving a trail of dust along the gravel road.

He was stronger than Garrett believed. He had his reasons for not talking about that dark part of his life. His chest tightened.

He scanned the area, searching for anything out of the ordinary. A shadow, a noise. Even silence that would hint at Carson's location. The asshole was close. He could almost sense him out there biding his time.

Kage slowly walked back toward the house to check on Jane. Garrett was right. He had to push away the past. Jane deserved more from him. But if Jane's safety came into play, he'd use whatever secret and connection he had to keep her safe, and he wouldn't regret a minute of it.

But he couldn't taint her with his past. When he was twenty-one, despite Jane knowing her own mind at seventeen, he'd believed he was doing the right thing by pushing her away. Then he'd worked years building a career for himself, staying in partnership with Garrett and the other guys, for the sole purpose of being near her. Hoping that, someday, she'd see him for who he really was:

A man with an ugly past who rose above the path of crime his family had paved for him.

A man who'd wrapped Jane's heart in the safety of his hands and now had made the decision to throw it away to keep her safe.

In the end, she'd see this move for what it was, the wrong direction. That was okay. She could end up hating him for the rest of her life, but she'd have a life.

Chapter Six

Kage's house would never be the same. He leaned against the archway leading into the kitchen, watching Jane stir a bowl of some creation she just had to make tonight. After a trip to the grocery store after work—because Jane declared she couldn't live off peanut-buttered toast and pretzels for two meals straight—he'd purchased enough groceries to feed three families.

She'd continued at a frantic pace, turning his kitchen into a world-class bakery, complete with a messy baker. He'd proceeded to stuff himself with samples as an excuse to hang out with her.

He found himself listening to her senseless babbling about how cowboy boots would never go out of style and if she won the lottery, she'd put a girls' bathroom in at the garage. Stupid shit he didn't even care about, but because it was important to her, he liked hearing her thoughts.

She moved with grace around the kitchen. As she did so, he shoved his hands in his front pockets, taking in the way she swept the stray strands of hair off her face. Every move she made was an erotic show. If he spent the rest of his life watching her, he'd always find something new to admire about the way she moved or tilted her head when she was concentrating on listening or the way her eyes narrowed when dirty filled her head.

Despite his feelings for her, he had no idea if she was ready to think about her future when her life was in danger. The emotional upheaval and the abuse she'd endured in the past meant he needed to step back and let her make the first move. The last thing he wanted was for her to misconstrue his feelings for her and think he acted on pity.

There were times she connected with him, and he was sure she understood where he was coming from. Then she'd retreat and deny she was feeling the same thing.

Yeah, he could practically read her mind at those times, and it infuriated her when she caught him grinning.

Although he'd done nothing physical tonight, his heart raced. His muscles were tense, and every time she passed him a treat, he got hard from the brush of her hand. If anyone could die from too much pleasure, he would've keeled over a half hour ago.

He sighed in contentment. The flour-covered counters, the handful of bowls he didn't even know he owned, and the woman scurrying between projects gave him a lot to look forward to. He lifted his glass of water and drank. He'd have to put in an extra hour of weights every day for the rest of the week. "I think you've made enough for one night," he offered.

Jane glanced at him over her shoulder. "One more batch of cookies, and then I have to clean up."

"Leave it." He pushed off the wall, walked toward her, and put his glass in the sink. "Come to bed."

"I can't." She threw the oven mitt on the counter. "I also need to wait until the brownies cool before I cut them up, and make more frosting for the sheet cake"—she slapped his hands away—"because you ate half the container of pre-made frosting we bought."

He studied her closely, and it finally dawned on him what the purpose of tonight's marathon baking stint was all about. "You're stalling."

"I like to bake." She reached around him and grabbed the dishtowel.

If she'd set out to stay busy to keep from going to bed with him, he could be patient. He had to admit he was a selfish man. He couldn't wait to get her beside him, wrapped in his arms. The last thing he wanted was her crashing when she finally hit the sheets. In bed was the one place she let down her defenses and opened up to him. He had the old Janie back who trusted him.

He took that moment to wrap his arms around her.

"What are you doing?" She gazed up at him. "I'm covered in flour."

"I need you to do something for me."

She blinked at him. "What?"

"Stand still for thirty seconds."

She opened her mouth. He put his finger on her lips. Being this close, holding her was almost too much.

He gazed into her eyes. "Thirty seconds."

She tapped her foot against the floor. He kept her waiting, enjoying the way she squirmed against him.

Then her body stilled. He lifted his hand and sank his fingers into her hair, walking her forward until she was pressed against the counter. He wasn't going to allow her to escape him this time.

"Is that all you want me to do? Stand still?" she whispered.

"Not by a long shot." He shook his head grinning. "I'm not going to wait until you kiss me, because you're taking too damn long."

"Oh."

He captured her lips. His hand sank deeper into her hair, pulling her toward him with enough pressure that she rose up on tiptoes as he deepened the kiss. This was no time for teasing, his need for her too great. It had been a long time coming, and he wasn't in the mood to mess around.

She leaned into him, grabbing the sides of his jeans. He stroked her tongue with his, tasting the sugary sweetness of all her baking mixed with the way he'd imagined she'd taste. No, *better* than he'd imagined.

He softened his mouth, slowed down, smiled through the kiss as her fingers dug into his sides and held on. He'd finally given her what she wanted seven years ago. Pulling her to him, he cupped her ass and supported her weight. The whole time he continued to stroke her, showing her what he wanted from her, she moaned. The verbal acceptance wrapped around him and he groaned his answer. Knowing he had to pace himself for her sake, but feeling he'd rather die than stop, he eased his head back and tucked her under his chin, holding her tight. His heart raced, and his balls ached.

"I wanted to do that for a long time," he whispered.

"I tried, but you sent me away," she whispered back.

He remembered. God, he remembered. "You were seventeen-year-old jailbait. I was twenty-one. I couldn't go there. You know me."

She leaned back. "Kage…"

"I want you in my life. I always have." He inhaled, held his breath, and let it out when he stepped away. "Clean up, finish whatever it is you're accomplishing here, and come to me." He studied her.

She stood where he left her. He swiped his tongue over his bottom lip, still tasting her. Then he turned and strolled out of the room. Halfway down the hall, Bluff walked out of the spare bedroom. Kage picked her up and carried her with him.

"Better give her some space, cat. If the real Janie is still there, the kitchen's going to be a dangerous place to be in a few—"

A clatter filled the house, followed by the oven door slamming shut and a frustrated squeal. He smiled and walked into the room. "Nailed that one."

After he settled Bluff on the bed, he took his laptop to the chair in the corner, propped his feet on the end of the bed, and powered on. Garrett had Jane's personal account forwarded to him through the agency's computer, so they could keep an eye on any communication from her ex-boyfriend. He hoped to get an idea of Carson's location through his Internet service provider.

An email message popped up and he clicked on it.

If I see you sleeping with that asshole again, you'll owe me, sweetheart. Soon. S.

His feet went to the floor, and he tossed the laptop onto the bed, grabbing his phone off the dresser to call the hotline.

"Yo." Lance answered.

"We've got a hot trail. Pull up Jane's email account and trace the ISP and any other info you can find. Make a record of the email." He stalked to the end table, turned out the light, then backed to the window. He peeled back the curtain and peered out into the darkness.

The floodlight from the old barn lit up the front yard. He scanned the road, the driveway, the vacant landscape.

The night was quiet, not even a shadow or a lone car coming down the lane. He focused in on the rhododendron bushes blocking the mailbox from the house. He should've cut them down months ago. The overgrown bushes were an eyesore but, more important, they were big enough to hide a small car.

"Got it. It's a phone service through a local tower. Hang on again." A series of beeps came over the phone.

Kage closed the drapes. "Put a call in to Garrett. I want backup."

"Already done." Lance cussed. "Okay, his phone's untraceable. He's using a prepaid throwaway."

"Figures." Kage picked up his gun off the dresser, shoved in into the back of his jeans. "I'm going out."

"Jane?" Lance asked.

"Kitchen. Tell Garrett I'm setting the alarm and he should meet me outside." He disconnected.

Kage slipped on his leather jacket as he made his way back into the kitchen. Jane turned, and he ducked as she threw a cookie in his direction.

"I know what you're trying to do." She glared. "It's not going to work a second time."

He shut off the kitchen light and walked toward her, knowing she'd be blind in the dark. Her surprise bought him a couple seconds of quiet.

"What are you—?"

He covered her mouth with his before releasing her quickly. "Quiet and listen. Can you do that?" When she nodded, he continued. "Scott contacted you by email, and there's a good chance he's found your location."

"How do you know that?" She grabbed onto his jacket.

"From what he wrote in the email to you. Lance hacked into your information a few days ago and is directing everything from your in-box to my laptop."

She gasped. He shushed her. "I'm going outside and taking a look around. I want you to follow the wall to your right and go into the living room. Do not turn on the lights. Understand?"

"Please don't go outside," she said. "You can't leave me, I'm scared."

"Listen to me. You'll be fine. Once I'm out, you'll set the alarm, and I'll be within distance to hear it if it goes off," he said. "I wouldn't leave you if I thought there was any way for him to get in the house without me noticing."

"I really need my gun back."

He shook his head. "No gun. Go. Clear your throat when you reach the front door and unarm the alarm. Then count to ten and reset it." He led her to the inside kitchen wall. "Then sit on the living room floor. Even if you hear anything, do not get up."

She shuffled her feet, working her way around the kitchen. He took out his pistol. She hesitated in the archway. "Go."

"Kage…be careful. You don't know what he's capable of."

That's where she was wrong. Kage knew exactly what Carson was capable of, and he'd do anything to make sure none of it touched Jane again. Kage had trained, experienced, and come out alive in more dangerous situations in his life. His chest tightened. But he'd never had Jane to protect before. He'd make damn sure they both survived.

"Kage?"

"Do what I tell you, Janie. Please."

She followed his directions and went into the living room. A few seconds later, she cleared her throat. He headed to the back door, slipped outside, and listened for any noise.

The crickets chirped, a frog croaked intermittently from the spring that ran a hundred yards behind his house. He was thankful for any noise to cover his movements, knowing Carson wouldn't recognize the sound of the night if it bit him in the ass. This was Kage's territory.

He'd grown up in this house. Only during the time he spent with the Dentons had he been away. Even then, he'd always come here to find a connection to family when life got too heavy, even though he knew how messed up that seemed to others. His parents had lost the property, but he'd bought it back the minute he earned enough money for a down payment.

The house stayed vacant for years. Nobody wanted a known drug dealer's house, let alone a place where someone overdosed and died. That was fine by him. Every day it reminded him of what he would not become. He was an Archer by birth, but he would not carry on that legacy.

Staying close to the building, his back to the wall, he scanned the perimeter. He planned to use the old barn to draw Carson away from the house, away from Jane, if he showed himself. He forged his way to the roadside to make sure Carson wasn't using the bushes to hide in.

While he made his way across the yard, he listened.

The crickets continued their incessant chirps. He eyed the distance to the mailbox, cleared the area safe, and ran to the closest rhododendron. Creeping along the side, he rolled around to the front, his pistol raised.

Nothing.

The area was clear.

Dammit. He sensed movement coming from his left, stilled, then relaxed at the familiar whistle.

Garrett approached him. "All clear for the quarter of a mile leading to the house."

"There's no sign that anyone's been here recently." Kage lifted his chin. "Barn."

With unspoken understanding, they separated, each going in a different direction. Since he knew the lay of the barn, Kage entered, knowing Garrett had his back.

Ten minutes later, he left the barn through the front double doors, swinging them wide open. He'd hear if anyone closed them later.

Garrett slipped his gun into his holster. "We'll get him."

"Not soon enough." Anxious to get back to Jane, he walked toward the house with Garrett at his side.

"How's Jane doing?" Garrett asked.

"The email shook her. Before that happened, she seemed to be acclimating pretty well." He saw no reason to share with Garrett the way she'd kissed him. "Every time I think of what she must've gone through…"

"I know."

He blew out a breath. "When we catch this bastard, I want ten minutes with him."

"Kage—"

"I'm not asking." He looked at Garrett. "I'll walk away from the agency afterward if that's what it comes down to but I'm taking my ten minutes, and that's still letting him off too easily."

Garrett nodded, putting a hand to his friend's shoulder. Kage peered up into the sky. He was tense and angry and he couldn't walk into the house in that condition. Jane had gone through enough.

"I'm sending Tony out in the field tomorrow morning. He'll find him." Garrett moved away. "I'll let him know the latest."

Forcing a calm he didn't really feel, Kage nodded, and turned toward the house.

A scream came from inside. Kage turned to Garrett, motioning for him to take the front, and put his hand on the doorknob. Adrenaline spiked. Motherfucker. It was locked.

He shoved his hand in his pocket, finding the key, and shoved the door open the second the lock turned. Jane screamed again, adding to the noise of the alarm going off. He hurried through the house, pistol drawn, eyes scanning the dark. He shoved away the panic pulsing in his veins.

He found her in the hallway after almost tripping over her. She grabbed his pant leg and tugged. He squatted and ran his hand along the length of her back.

"Oh God, you've got to help me." She dragged herself up his body.

Fear that Carson had gotten to her pierced his chest. He wrapped his arm around her, pulling her tight against him. He raised his other hand, the pistol aimed into the dark. *Show yourself, you stupid bastard. Come on.*

Chapter Seven

Kage pulled Jane down the hall, through the house into the living room, turning on the lights as they went, without ever letting go of her. Jane fisted his jacket, shaking him. "Please, I know you want to keep me safe, but I need your help."

All the times Scott had come after her, she'd managed to keep her promise to Bluff that she'd keep her safe and not let Scott hurt her again. She couldn't screw up now. She blinked against the light and pushed Kage away.

He caught her arm and pulled her back. She landed against his chest.

"Talk to me," he said.

"Not now." She tried to step back, but Kage wasn't letting her go. "I have to find Bluff."

"Bluff?" Kage went rigid.

She nodded, scanning the room, under the couch, behind the wooden rocker. "That's what I've been trying to tell you. She's missing."

"You screamed because you can't find the damn cat?" His voice took on a hard tone.

"Her name's Bluff." She pushed herself from him, ready to beg if she had to convince him to find the cat first before they tried figuring anything else out. "Please. I can't let anything happen to her. She's already been through so much."

Garrett slipped his pistol into his waistband. "Sis? The cat will come out. Give her time."

"Janie..." Kage began.

"*No!*" She shook her head. "You don't understand. She hides or runs when she's scared."

"I'll take care of this," Kage muttered to Garrett.

She ignored the two guys and hurried down the hall. "Here, kitty, kitty, kitty."

If Jane could keep Bluff safe, she'd do anything Kage asked her to do. She'd cooperate and stay out of trouble while he went after Scott. As long as she had Bluff, and they were both okay, she could push the real threat of Scott coming after her tonight out of her head.

Boxes filled the first spare room on her left. She squatted, looking between the stacks. "Bluff...I have tuna..."

She blew her bangs out of her eyes and moved to the next room. With only a chair and a couple of small toolboxes set against the wall, she quickly realized the cat wasn't there. She checked the bathroom, the linen closet, the hall closet where the sliding door had been left partially opened. Bluff loved to nap in tiny, dark places.

She swallowed the panic. What if Bluff had managed to slip outside when Kage had gone out to look around?

"Kage!" She turned, colliding with him. "We have to—"

"Here." He strode toward her and placed the cat in her arms. "She was outside, hunkered behind the bush by the front door. I found her after Garrett secured the premises. I've set the alarm."

Relief swept through Jane. She clung to Bluff, holding the cat beneath her chin, and sank to the floor, rocking her. "I'm sorry. I'll never let you out of my sight again." She closed her eyes against the tears. "We're okay, Bluff. Everything is okay. Kage saved you. He'll keep us both safe."

She stroked Bluff, who seemed undisturbed from their time apart. Jane continued to lavish the animal with attention, consoling herself as much as the feline. She opened her eyes and saw Kage's boots planted right in front of her. Her resolve crumbled.

He slid his hands under her arms and picked her and Bluff up in one swoop. His jaw ticked, but his eyes remained focused on Jane. In her relief at having Bluff back and knowing everything was okay, she'd forgotten he was watching her.

"I'm…I'm sorry." She broke his gaze. "Thanks for looking out for Bluff. If anything would've happened to her, I'd never have forgiven myself."

"Jane. Look at me." He relaxed his stance. "Everything is okay, inside and out."

"That's good, right?"

"Yeah, baby, that's good." He inhaled deeply. "It's late. Let's relax, maybe watch a little television before we go to sleep."

She bit down on her lower lip and glanced behind her. "I need to clean the—"

"Jane." He stooped to look her straight in the eyes. "You need to rest. Let me take care of you for a change. Go take a shower. While you're doing whatever girls do, I'll take care of all the food you made and load the dishwasher. Then I'll check if there's a movie on TV, and we can stretch out on the bed and relax."

She nodded, needing the escape. The tenderness emanating from Kage unsettled her. She wanted him but had no right to become involved with him. Her judgment needed realigning. She'd fallen for Scott because he'd made her feel safe at one time. Maybe she had a thing for possessive, dominant men.

Kage studied her and she melted. No, Kage was different. He was confident and supportive where Scott chewed her up and spat her out. Kage never made her feel stupid the way Scott did. She hated those feelings she lived with for so long. "Okay."

"Good." He stepped aside, and she hurried past him into the bedroom. After depositing Bluff onto the bed, she grabbed her pajama shorts and camisole off her pillow and shut herself in the bathroom, eager to settle in beside Kage for the night.

In the shower, she scrubbed her hair extra hard, quickly lathered her body, and then stood under the spray of the water only long enough to rinse the soap off. She couldn't scrub away the terror she'd felt watching Kage walk away, thinking he might never come back.

What if he found out the truth about the stolen money and left her to face Scott alone? She lowered her chin to her chest and let the water wash over her. Kage promised he'd help. She'd have to find a way to make sure she was there if Scott showed himself.

Scott's agenda had been to keep her around to have someone handy to abuse. He'd want Kage out of the picture, so he could make her pay for leaving him. If anything happened to him, it'd be her fault. And that was something she couldn't face.

The only way to prove to Kage that she could handle this on her own and get him and the other boys to back off was to get stronger. She'd show him that she could take care of herself. She wouldn't allow Scott to hurt anyone else. But first, she needed a gun.

She stepped out of the shower, dried off, and put on her night-clothes. She toweled the drips out of her hair, leaving it uncombed and wet, and went out into the bedroom. She let out a relieved breath. Kage was still cleaning.

Seizing the opportunity, she snatched her phone off the dresser and checked her messages. If Scott had sent her anything, maybe she could delete it before someone at headquarters noticed and transferred the message to Kage. To stay one step ahead of the boys, she'd have to think like them.

Sabrina had left another message. The urge to see her friend outweighed the embarrassment of coming clean. She texted Sabrina, setting up a lunch date at the garage for Saturday, hoping her friend wouldn't hate her. They hadn't seen each other in four years, except for a brief time at her dad's funeral. It was safer that way.

Maybe when all her troubles no longer existed, the friendships she'd had before could return to normal. A pang of regret over lost time never went away. Who was she fooling?

She hated how she'd allowed herself to fall into an unhealthy relationship, stripping her of all her confidence. Scott's rants were all too true. She *was* pathetic.

There were no messages from him. She set the phone on the nightstand, shut off the light, and stretched out on top of the bed.

And waited.

In what seemed like hours, but by her phone was only thirty minutes, Kage still hadn't returned to the bedroom. Yawning, she turned and pulled his pillow to her. She hugged it to her chest and inhaled, eyes closed.

Her stomach fluttered. She couldn't even describe the scent. It was just Kage. The man who offered her comfort, security, and more stubbornness than she knew what to do with. And most of all, he was familiar.

There were many nights she'd lain in the same bed as Scott, reciting the phone number Kage had given her, wishing it was he who had fallen in love with her. Afraid Scott would find out, she went to great pains never to mention anyone from her past. Kage was her lifeline. She could handle one more day with Scott, because she knew in her heart if things got worse, Kage would be there for her if she called.

But she hadn't called. She could never find the strength to admit that she'd failed.

Kage's strength overshadowed her. She wasn't good enough for him anymore, and she couldn't understand why he'd kissed her earlier—kissed her as if he never wanted to stop. If only she hadn't met Scott, then maybe she'd stand a chance, maybe she could let herself go and fall for Kage.

The bed dipped. Too tired to move, she lay there until Kage tugged his pillow from her grasp and pulled her against his side. Her head lay on his bare chest. He was warm and solid. She threw her arm across his stomach and snuggled in. Several minutes passed, and she felt herself slipping into sleep.

"Janie?" he whispered.

Her body seized and now she was fully awake. "Don't call me that."

"You'll always be Janie to me." He kissed the top of her head.

"Janie doesn't exist anymore." Immediately after uttering the words, she regretted them. She sighed and laid her head back down. Why couldn't he understand that the person he'd called Janie so many years ago no longer existed. "This is humiliating."

"No reason for it," he murmured. "You're not responsible for what someone else is doing to you."

"I could've stopped him." She grimaced. "You should really let me go back home. Garrett can watch out for me."

"No." His arm tightened around her. "You don't get it. You're here. You're in my bed. You're not leaving."

She wasn't going to argue. Tomorrow she'd figure a way out of this mess and out of Kage's life. She could deal with him being mad at her. It was the kindness, the concern, the warmth, the kiss—those things, she couldn't handle.

"Why Bluff?" he asked.

She opened her eyes. "What?"

"Why were you scared when you thought Bluff was lost?"

"It doesn't matter," she mumbled.

She pushed away from him, rolled, and gave him her back. He turned with her, tagging her waist and pulling her back to spoon. She held her breath, waiting for him to make a move, but he only held her.

"Why Bluff?" he whispered, not giving up.

She swallowed. "Bluff's a stray. When I found her, she was all scratched up and had a big gash on her neck that was infected. I took her in, cleaned and treated her wounds, and have had her ever since."

"For how long?"

"Two years," she said.

His fingers sprawled on her stomach. "You've kept her safe."

She nodded.

"Why does she need to be protected?" he asked.

The last thing she wanted to do was try to explain to Kage how much Bluff meant to her. Yes, Bluff was a cat, but she was also so much more. At times, Bluff kept her sane. During the worst periods, Bluff loved her even when she knew no one else would.

"Answer me, Janie."

His tone left little choice but to respond. "Scott. Bluff needed protection from Scott."

"Fuck," he bit off. "What happened?"

"I don't want to talk about it." She turned onto her back. In the dark, she could face him.

His body went tight. "Tell me what happened."

She could handle the fighting, the broken things Scott hurled across the room that she'd brought with her into the relationship, and the words he threw at her. Even the shoves and broken ribs.

She'd never forgive the times he attacked Bluff because he knew it would hurt her worse than any beating.

"He used her against me. He thought nothing of kicking or throwing her across the room if he caught me holding her on my lap when he got home. He was jealous of the attention I gave her. I tried to be so careful. I'd lock her in the basement with my robe, so she could sleep in peace and still be able to have a part of me. But I never knew when Scott would show up at the house. One time he locked her outside." She inhaled deeply. "I thought she'd run away, because really, no one wants to live where someone hurts them. I wouldn't have blamed her if she wanted a new home, and honestly, I wanted her to run. I hoped she'd run far away and some little girl, with loving parents, would take her in."

She smiled. "Bluff would love a little girl to take care of her and dress her up. She's very easygoing, don't you think?"

"Yeah, baby."

She lowered her voice. "Bluff hid behind the bush by the front door. For some reason she stayed for me, so I promised I'd protect her."

"Bluff loves you." He stroked her hair away from her face. "Sometimes it's as simple as that."

"If anything happens to me—"

"Nothing is going to happen," he said.

"Listen to me. Please." She grabbed his hand and linked their fingers together, holding tight. "If Scott wins, you have to promise me you'll take care of Bluff. Please. That's all that matters. She's had a rough life. She doesn't deserve to be homeless again."

Kage leaned down, put his head beside hers, his mouth on her ear. "I promise, but nothing will happen to you."

She nodded, swallowing down the tears. She would not cry.

Instead, she snuggled closer. "Can you just hold me?"

"You never have to ask me for that, babe. It's a given." He kissed her softly. "Close your eyes and rest."

That light brush of his lips. The softness she had never experienced broke something inside of her. She rolled back toward him and put her head on his chest, her arm around his stomach.

He curled his arm around her, his hand landing on her hip. The flutter in her stomach returned with a vengeance, and she tilted her head. "Kage, about the kiss…"

"Yeah?"

"We shouldn't do that anymore," she said.

"Trust me, we'll do more than kiss." He found humor in her suggestion, because his chest quivered under her cheek. "Now go to sleep, Janie."

"Stop calling me that," she whispered.

"I'm not going to give in to you about that…Janie." He propped himself on his elbow. "The woman I knew is still in there. I see her. You feel her. I'll be damned if I'll let you throw her away as if she's not important. There was a time when I gave up on myself, and if it hadn't been for you, I wouldn't be here with you now. I want you, and I know you to want me. And it will happen soon."

"W-what does that mean?" She gulped, knowing exactly what he wanted from her and excited over the thought of being with him completely.

"Use your imagination." He fell back on the bed, wrapped himself around her, and held her tight. "For now, get some rest. We have a busy day tomorrow."

Rest? He expected her to rest after the direction their conversation had taken? She tapped his arm. "Kage?"

He chuckled. "What?"

He was right. She *did* want something from him, but more important, she needed to prove she was strong enough to give Kage more of herself. Her chest tightened, and she realized he was right. She had to admit out loud that the real Janie inside of her still existed. Scott hadn't ruined her, and she wanted everything Kage reminded her of and more. "I just wanted to tell you I changed my mind. You can call me Janie."

For a few seconds she thought he wasn't going to reply. Then he captured her cheeks and kissed her hard. He took what she offered him and deepened the kiss. Dizzy, she closed her eyes, letting the rush of pleasure sweep through her. Unable to move, because all her muscles had liquefied, all her senses had heightened as he slowly stroked, sucked, and eased away from her with the gentlest lips, caressing the embers of the fire he'd created inside her.

When he laid his forehead against hers, she blew out her breath. "Wow."

"Yeah, baby. It feels like I've wanted you for a lifetime." He threw his leg across her thigh. "Once this is all over, you'll see. Me. You. Can't fucking wait."

That decided it. She smiled against his neck. No one would stop her from being with Kage. And she would make the first move...tomorrow.

Chapter Eight

Jane paced the living room holding Bluff, waiting for Kage to finish in the bathroom. She glanced at her purse, and wondered if she had time to put Kage's pistol back in the dresser drawer.

"He's going to kill me," she whispered to Bluff.

Bluff meowed, pushing her paws against Jane's chest. She held on tighter. It was too late. He could come out at any time and catch her in the act. How was she going to explain why she stole his weapon?

No. She blew out her breath and resumed her pacing. She had to do it this way. Let him think someone else broke in, or he misplaced it. She could tell him during last night's chaos with Scott sending her a message, him going outside, and her hysteria over thinking she'd lost Bluff, he must have left the pistol outside.

"Jane!" Kage called from the bedroom.

Shit. She set Bluff on the couch. "Yeah?"

"Get in here."

Uh-oh. She walked down the hallway and stood in front of the bedroom doorway. "What's up?"

Deciding to play it loose, she leaned against the door frame. She raised her brow as if she was clueless over why he glared at her from the middle of the room, or why his jaw muscle twitched. Her independence meant she had to stay strong.

"Where's my gun?"

She lifted her shoulder. "Isn't it in the drawer?"

"You know it's not." He stepped forward. "You have half a second to tell me where it is."

Pissed off didn't describe Kage. Anger rolled off him and consumed the empty space in the room. Jane walked toward him, shook her head, and passed him on the way to the bathroom. At the door, she faced him again. "I really have no idea where your gun is, Kage. Maybe look in the kitchen. You might've put it there last night when you came inside."

He growled.

"I'm going to put my makeup on, and then I'll be ready to go." She turned and closed the door.

She slumped forward, holding onto the counter. *Please, please, please don't check my purse.*

Barely able to look herself in the mirror, she decided to put on smoky charcoal eyeliner, mascara, a swipe of lipstick. She rubbed her lips together while searching for her earrings she set on the counter last night. After moving Kage's shaving cream, hair brush, razor, the dirty towel he'd left out, she looked along the floor in case he'd accidentally knocked them off.

The silver hoops were too big to go down the drain. She stood and went out of the bathroom. She'd have to remember to go through her old jewelry box in her room during lunch and see if there was anything in there she could wear without bouncing back a decade. Naked ears drove her nuts.

Jane entered the living room and spotted Kage standing in front of the window, his back to her. "Hey, did you notice a pair of earrings in the bathroom earlier?"

He turned and shook his head. "No."

Shit. He was still mad. She glanced at her purse. It sat in the same spot she'd left it in, on the couch. "Bummer. I thought I'd put them on the counter…maybe I took them off at work."

"Let's go. We're late." He strode to the door and waited for her.

She leaned over the couch, air-kissed Bluff, gave the cat a couple of strokes from head to tail, picked up her purse, and walked to the door. She waited for him to key in the alarm.

"One second, while I scan the yard." Kage opened the door, stepped outside, looked around, and then motioned for her to come outside. She stood between him and the house, while he reached over her shoulder and set the alarm again before quickly shutting the door to beat the time limit.

He followed the same ritual as yesterday. She moved close to him, keeping her purse opposite of him. He pulled her close as they hurried to the car. She knew he hadn't found the gun; her purse weighed heavy with the bulk of the pistol.

Out on the main road, he stopped behind a school bus. She glanced at Kage. They were forty-five minutes late, but that was okay since the shop had irregular business hours. She had to admit she enjoyed working days instead of alone at night, and found herself slowly forgetting about her problems during the busy hours at the garage.

The constant camaraderie among the boys put her at ease, and she looked forward to the many times Kage visited her in the office between car jobs. He'd pushed his investigation cases onto the others to spend all his time with her, and though that was one more thing for her to feel guilty about, she loved having him around.

The school bus took off, and Kage flipped on his turn signal, passed in the other lane, and drove on. She decided a distraction from her fascination with Kage called for a break or she'd never make it through the day. "Can you walk me into my house during lunch or after work, so I can grab some of my old clothes? I still haven't found time to go shopping."

He kept his gaze on the road. "Yeah."

She fingered the leather material of her purse strap. He'd barely said two words during the drive, and she had a feeling he was waiting for her to confess to stealing his gun. She gazed out the window. Once they arrived at the garage, she hoped he'd get another pistol or realize she had a valid reason for wanting to carry one herself.

Kage drove past the house and parked behind Beaumont Body and Shop. She waited until he exited the car and retrieved her, simply because it pleased him when he could do the simple things like opening her car door for her.

As he opened the door she slid off the seat to the ground, but he blocked her from going any further, pinning her against the car.

"I'll make sure to walk you over to the house." He gazed intently at her and kissed her.

As always, he didn't beat around the bush, and she wondered if this was his way of making her believe he forgot about the gun. Was he just biding his time before confronting her again? The kiss was hot and heavy, stealing her thoughts. She enjoyed the feel of his hard body pressed against her. As she felt the urgent proof of how much he looked forward to seeing her tonight, pleasant tingles swirled and dipped low between her legs. Just as she turned to leave him, he stopped her.

"Janie?" He gazed into her eyes. "Don't you have anything to tell me?"

She squashed down the guilt over stealing from him and told him a different truth. "Yes. I can't wait to see you tonight."

She rose up on her toes and kissed him. Tonight was the night, and not because he pressured her into being with him, but because she cared for him and loved how give gave her the space she needed to move at her own speed. She longed to have sex with him and to let go of her past. They'd created a new beginning, and she knew he wouldn't turn her away this time.

She accepted everything he gave her, and her body craved all the things he could do for her. His hand came up to her head, held her there. He moved his mouth along her lips, her cheek, and settled on her ear.

"Don't deny it. You're my woman. You've always been mine," he murmured in her ear, his voice rougher than she'd ever heard it.

Her brain fizzled. She was no longer running away, but straight to him. She let him take her hand and lead her to the back door. Once inside, she scurried down the hall into the body shop, leaving him somewhere back near the holding rooms. Alone in the office, she shut the door and touched her lips. How was she supposed to follow through with her plan when he was making it impossible to walk away?

For one long moment back there, and many more times over the last several days, he'd tempted her to abandon her fears and fall all over his offer. She shook her head. Jumping into bed with the first person who made her feel desirable had gotten her in trouble the first time.

She'd given her all to Scott only to have him beat her and take away the security she'd felt at the beginning of their relationship. She knew Kage would never hurt her, but it was hard to let go of all her past hurt so quickly.

How could she become strong enough not to lose herself again when Kage encompassed her whole being? He literally had the power to destroy her.

To keep herself from worrying about her seduction, she plunged right into work. For the next two hours, she billed insurance companies, ordered parts, and called the repair tech to come out and look at the spare air compressor in stall 3. After she completed a few more calls to current customers, she looked for the invoices from yesterday and couldn't find them.

She unlocked the door to look for Garrett, hesitated, and walked back to get her purse. It wouldn't do to leave a loaded gun around if a customer came into the garage.

Out in the bays, the doors were down and the boys were missing. She headed back the way she'd come and turned toward the door to the agency. If Garrett wanted her to keep everything in order, he'd have to make sure she received the invoices the day the papers were due to be recorded.

Pushing through headquarters door, she was greeted by laughter. Garrett sat on the edge of a desk, his head thrown back. Lance held his earpiece in the air, cracking up. Tony stood off by the screens, a huge smile on his face. She turned to Kage, who was glaring at Garrett.

"What's so funny?" She let the door swing shut as she stepped inside the room.

The laughter dropped off abruptly. She looked around. None of the boys seemed eager to share the source of their amusement. She looked briefly at the ceiling. Whatever.

"How's it going?" Lance grinned.

"Uh…fine." She frowned at him.

Tony crossed his arms and rocked back on his heels "Going somewhere?"

She tilted her head and glanced behind her, following his gaze. "No. Why?"

"Go to hell, Tony." Kage swept his phone off the counter, ignoring her.

Garrett smacked his lips. "Damn. I can still taste the onion in that breakfast burrito. Do you have a breath mint, sis?"

"Yeah." She took her purse off her shoulder.

"Jane. Don't," Kage said.

She glanced at him, digging in her purse for the box of mints. "It's okay. I have enough."

"Hell," he muttered.

Geez, what was his problem? She slid her fingers around the pistol, searching the corner of her purse, then stilled. Heat rushed to her face. She fingered the cold metal, taking in the flat long shape, ending in a half moon she'd recognize in the dark if she were blind and wearing gloves.

Fury filled her and her gaze snapped to Kage. His eyes grew soft, and a look came over his face she read as half regret, half pissed-off male.

"You son of a bitch," she mumbled.

The boys picked up the mood and moved toward her. She pulled out the wrench Kage must've placed in her purse this morning after finding his gun and held it in the air.

"Stand back or I'll whack any one of you who comes near me," she said.

Chapter Nine

Jane's threats of hitting the men with the wrench had no effect on Garrett as he continued toward her. Kage looked on, hurting for his Janie. Her temper, her feistiness, her smart mouth were what he remembered and loved about her most. Jane's spirit set her apart from all other women. But at this moment, as much as he wanted to see the fire in her eyes, he regretted the other men egging her on.

The quiet, tame woman who'd returned to Bay City was the shell that Scott Carson threw away. Kage had wanted to bring the real Janie back, show her he had control of the situation. That he would catch the bastard and protect her.

Instead, he'd humiliated her by taking back his pistol and putting the damn wrench in her purse. He was going to bash heads once he was alone with Garrett, Tony, and Lance. They had no reason to make Jane feel like a fool.

"Give it back." Jane slapped at Garrett as he grabbed the wrench from her hand.

Garrett held the tool behind him. "Why don't you let Kage do his job?"

"Because he can't!" she spat, flashing her gaze to Kage.

Her body stiffened, and then her shoulders sagged. He schooled his reaction to her words. He'd heard the same thing growing up.

His dad, mom—before she overdosed—his uncle Darrell. He wasn't like them, and they found him lacking because he could see the difference between right and wrong. He'd spent his life proving he was nothing like the rest of the Archers. He continually fought the truth that the blood running through his veins matched that of people who used, abused, and killed.

He didn't poison others' minds with drugs, kill because that was the easiest answer, and he sure in the hell didn't work for his uncle. He continued watching her, begging her silently to explain her opinion. She made no move toward him; it seemed she'd said all she had to say.

He'd worked his entire adult life to prove to himself that he was strong enough to fight any temptation, greed, and addiction that came his way. To be the polar opposite of his father, mother, and uncle. Yet Jane shouted her doubts about the very thing he fought so hard for, and it hurt.

Only one person's opinion truly mattered, and he'd failed her.

Jane's warm brown eyes appeared to liquefy. She sucked in her bottom lip. Her breasts rose and fell with her emotional outburst. A strand of her ginger hair fell across her face, and she brushed it out of the way and stepped forward.

She'd deny that she had her doubts, because she knew that's what he wanted to hear. His back stiffened and he shifted his gaze away from her. He had to get out of there.

"Keep an eye on her." He didn't wait for confirmation but strode out the door.

He passed his car, no destination in mind, focused only on outrunning the knowledge that Jane didn't trust him. The absolute horror in her expression once she realized what she'd said stabbed him in the heart. He understood where she was coming from.

She'd been through her own nightmare. But, dammit, he had the power to help her, and he hated that couldn't make her feel safe.

At the edge of the parking lot he came to a stop. There was something he *could* do to put an immediate end to Jane's problem, to heal her and put Carson away for good.

His vow to stay far away from his relatives took the backseat when it came to Jane. From here on out, she came first in his life. He'd do what needed to be done to make sure she remained safe.

He pulled out his phone, scrolled down his contacts, and made the call.

"Yeah?" Darrell said.

He closed his eyes and let his chin fall forward. The smart thing to do was hang up. He knew the guys would stop at nothing to help him catch Scott. Asking his uncle for help went against everything he believed in. If he stepped over the line, he'd destroy what little trust Janie still had in him.

He disconnected the call.

The one thing he swore he'd never do, he'd done. His heart hammered. Bile rose in his throat. He felt sick over admitting he needed help from the one person he despised, yet knowing he'd do whatever it took to keep Jane safe left him empty and angry. After all these years, Darrell's voice remained strong, conveyed his power straight to the marrow of Kage's bones.

He couldn't ask for help yet. He wasn't out of options, but if it came down to it, he'd do what he had to. He only hoped he had enough information stored on his uncle to walk away when this was over. If he'd learned anything in his life, he knew better than to let Darrell hold a marker on him.

Determined not to think about what he'd almost done, Kage

returned to the office. He stood inside headquarters, his gaze immediately going to Jane. She looked him up and down before settling on his eyes.

He stepped forward, and Garrett moved in front of him. "What are you doing?"

"Taking care of business and making sure Janie stays safe. The same way you are." He walked around Garrett to his desk and sat down. "If things escalate with Scott, I'll have to bring one of you in to stay with Janie at all times."

"Kage." Garrett's voice held warning. "Tell me you didn't…"

He raised his chin. "I'm looking after Janie's safety the way I promised."

"Damn you. This is fucked up. If you know something you aren't telling us, it puts everyone at risk. You do not get to keep information to yourself. Spit it out," Garrett said.

Kage threw a look at Garrett. No one would talk him out of taking care of what was his, and he dared anyone to say Jane wasn't just that. In time, Garrett would come around to understanding this was what Jane needed, if nothing else. For now, the guys only needed to know he'd protect Jane with his life.

"Nothing's changed. Janie's at my house, you two are searching every corner for Carson, and Garrett is hanging around here in case he shows up looking for her," Kage said. "No one lets up."

"We'll meet in the morning." Lance shoved back in his chair. "I've got a lead across town I want to check out."

The tension in Garrett's shoulders remained and his gaze never wavered from Kage's. "I know something is going on in your head, and it's giving me a bad feeling."

"It's Carson. He can ruin anyone's mood." Kage stood, deciding there was nothing left to say. The other guys had his back. If push came to shove and he had to make right with his uncle, he'd walk before taking them down with him. "If anyone has something to say, tell me now, because in two minutes I'm going to walk Jane across the parking lot to her house, and then we're going home."

"Kage, I don't have to go to the house right now if you want to stay here," Jane said.

"I'm done here." He grabbed his jacket. "Let's go."

Jane turned, looking to her brother. Garrett glanced at him over her shoulder. Kage lifted his chin, daring him to put a stop to his plan. Brother or not, Garrett knew Kage would fight anyone who stepped in his way.

Garrett lowered his gaze to Jane and spoke to her quietly. Then he nodded at Kage. It was set. Kage would get no trouble from Garrett, and that meant the agency stood behind him with Jane too.

Kage held the door, and Jane slowly went out, staring up into his face. Together they walked to the house she'd lived in with her dad and brother.

She was silent, lost in her thoughts, and knowing her the way he did, she was probably listing each question she'd pepper him with later in alphabetical order. He opened the back door, and when she put her purse on the kitchen counter, he held up his hand. "Stay here. I want to make sure the house is secure."

Once he found no threat of Scott, he returned. "Get whatever you came for, so we can head back."

She stayed beside him. "Can we talk first?"

"No. Let's get done and go." He pulled out a chair and sat. Mentally exhausted, he raised his arms and clasped his hands behind his head. He refused to look away from Jane, hoping she'd retreat and not push him. Though he hated admitting he might need help dealing with Jane and Darrell at the same time. "Ten minutes, Jane."

Her mouth tightened, yet she walked away without giving him any lip. Once she was out of the room, Kage rubbed his hands over his face. If he agreed to bring in family, it meant he couldn't go forward with Jane. Tonight's plan to do more than sleep beside her was a bust if he made the wrong decision.

A thump followed by a curse came from the other end of the house. Kage rose and walked toward the sound of her voice. In the door to her room, he paused at the sight.

Jane leaned into the closet, her hands above her head, outfits piled on her arms, trying to keep the clothes from falling to the floor. "The rod broke."

"I can see that." He tilted his head, taking in the situation. "How?"

"I leaned against it to get to the top shelf. Help me before they all fall off and I have to rehang everything." Her face was red from struggle.

"The bracket broke." He reached above her and grabbed onto the bar. "Why didn't you yell if you needed help reaching the shelf?"

"Because I used to grab hold of it all the time when I lived here." She straightened the clothes that'd fallen off and hung them back up.

He leaned back without losing his grip on the bar. "You're bigger than you were years ago."

"What?" She swung around and glared at him.

He chuckled. "It's a good thing, baby. More curves to hold on to."

"I-I…" She blinked rapidly. "Are you calling me fat? Because for your information I weigh the same as I did when I graduated college."

"Perfect." He ogled her breasts. "You're in great shape."

Five feet six inches, slim waist, and breasts that he knew would overfill his hands. He leaned down and kissed her. His body reacted instantly, and suddenly he was harder than the closet rod he was holding. He couldn't wait to show her exactly how he felt about her body.

She whispered, "Okay then, I believe you."

He grinned, shoving the hangers away from the end of the bar. "Do you know where your dad kept a hammer, maybe a few nails? I can brace the bar until Garrett picks up another bracket."

"Yeah, in the garage he has a workbench with all his tools. I'll be right back." She moved.

"Hey, wait." He turned his gaze toward her. "Only go in the garage. Don't go outside."

She nodded and left.

Ten minutes later, he rigged the rod temporarily until Garrett could replace the bracket, removed the box from the upper shelf, and stood watching her. She sorted a pile of clothes and boots on her bed and stood picking through a jewelry box on her dresser. His chest tightened.

The white box covered with ladybugs matched her bedroom. A bedroom that'd seen her through growing up in the Beaumont house and retained the decorations of a happy childhood. She'd had everything he didn't growing up in a family who loved her unconditionally. H wanted her to have that normal, happy life again where she was able to enjoy reading in bed or worrying about what she was going to wear on a date when he took her out on the town. Everyone, especially her, deserved memories of a happier time. Call him selfish, but he wanted to experience those feelings with her.

"Did you bring anything with you when you came back from Pullman?" he asked.

Her shoulders stiffened and she stayed with her back toward him. "My Duster that dad gave me when I got my license, a couple changes of clothes, Scott's gun, one hundred thousand dollars, and Bluff."

His mind homed in on one thing. "I hope you had a fancy-ass job that allowed you to save that much money."

She shrugged. "He owes me, Kage. Big-time. It serves him right to lose the money. I more than earned that amount after putting up with his shit."

"Fuck." He rubbed the back of his neck. "Please tell me you went to a bank and withdrew it."

"No, he never used a bank." She dumped the jewelry she'd picked out into a bag and tossed it on the pile of clothes. "It's my money too. I worked and paid the bills, the rent, and bought my own clothes. He never gave me money, unless he bought me a gift. But he sure had no problem taking it over the years."

"Shit, Jane. You stole his money." He shook his head.

"I know." Jane shoved her belongings into a bag. "I screwed up big-time. I never thought I'd have you and Garrett involved in this mess. My only concern was getting away and making it back to Bay City."

"Drug money," he muttered. He took the bag out of her hands. "You didn't steal money he earned or took from you. You stole dirty money, and someone will want that money back. Probably Carson, but if not him, then the person who hired him."

Her brows rose. "That's why I took the money. Don't you see? I'm not stupid. That money is going to keep me safe. Scott wouldn't dare kill me if he has no idea where I hid the money. He'll want to keep me alive, because he probably has to give the money back to the supplier. He's greedy, and won't like dipping into his own cash. I know I'm not worth anything to him."

"Dammit, Janie, it doesn't work that way." Kage grabbed her hand, pulling her through the house.

She hurried to keep up with his pace. "Kage, wait. If it's someone else's money, I'll give it back. I only took it to get even with Scott and to keep him from hurting me."

He led her outside, scanned the area, and then pulled her across the way. "Right now we're going to go tell the guys this new information, and then I'm taking you home and hopefully keeping you out of more trouble."

Kage knew Carson wasn't working alone, not if he had that much money available. He answered to someone bigger and more powerful. This information put a new angle on the situation. Kage had a bad feeling that if Scott was working with that heavy a purse, his uncle would be his only link to finding out what in the hell was going on.

Because nothing happened in the area that Darrell Archer wasn't aware of, and most times his hand was in play.

When push came to shove, he hoped the four of them were big enough to deal with the situation. Who knew how big it would get before they were through?

Chapter Ten

Kage deposited Jane in a holding room with Garrett, to give them privacy, and left. She threw up her hands and sank down on the edge of the bed. Her outlook on life had changed. Things were a lot worse now because of the stolen money.

Her only thought at the time was escape. She covered her face with her hands and groaned. Now Garrett and Kage were mad, and they had every right to be. In her frantic need to leave, she hadn't considered what Scott would do when he found his money missing. It had seemed so simple when she'd planned everything.

She raised her gaze to Garrett. "I'm sorry. I keep putting everyone in more danger, and that wasn't my intent. I only wanted to get away from Scott. Now I'm afraid Kage is going to do something he regrets. I need to talk with him."

"Let him do his job," Garrett said.

"How was I supposed to know someone besides Scott would be looking for the money?" She moistened her lips. There had to be a way to fix everything. "What if we use the money to draw Scott out into the open? Maybe I can talk to him, and while he's distracted, you guys catch him. We can call the police and I'll press charges. This time I won't chicken out."

Garrett frowned. She continued. "I only wanted to start over and leave the life I had with him behind. I wanted to come home, Garrett. You have to understand, I wasn't thinking straight."

"Think. That's all I'm asking you to do." Garrett crossed his arms in front of the door. "Is there anything else you haven't told us?"

"Like what?" she said.

"Oh, I don't know, sis, but you haven't given us the whole story yet." Garrett inhaled deeply. "Listen. You and I are the only ones left in the family. You were too little to remember, but before Mom died, she made us all promise to love and take care of each other. I'm trying...now that Dad's gone, you're all I got. Do you know what it does to me to hear Scott was selling drugs around you and sticking a fucking pistol in your mouth?"

She sniffed and closed her eyes for a beat and whispered, "I know."

"Can you remember seeing anyone meeting with Scott, or anyone his men might have referred to when they talked business?"

"No." She shook her head. "They never used names. M-maybe I can describe them. They were big, about your size, a-and they never looked at me directly. Scott wouldn't allow them to look at me. Most of the time I ignored what was happening, because it was easier than accepting it."

"Did you ever think to tell me...your brother? I would've helped you."

She let her chin fall to her chest.

Garrett was pissed. He took his responsibility as her older brother seriously, and she not only hurt him, she'd broken the bond they both clung to desperately. She stood and approached him. "I'm sorry."

"You have to stop protecting him," he said quietly.

She rocked back. "I'm not!"

"Are you sure?"

The fact that he questioned her at all hurt. She went back to the bed and sat. None of them understood. It wasn't Scott she was protecting. It was Kage, Garrett, and the rest of the boys.

"When I came home, I didn't even want to tell you why I came back." She stared at Garrett. "You'd been through so much already dealing with Dad, and I wasn't here to help."

Garrett was stepping toward her when the door swung open.

Charlene strode through in all her glistening rhinestones adorning her short skirt and blouse. Ignoring Garrett, she went straight to Jane, who found herself wrapped in Charlene's arms, her head pulled to the older woman's ample breasts. Even though she was frustrated at everyone, she couldn't deny that it felt good to have someone hold her.

"I walk into the garage, find no one around, and almost got shot by Lance." Charlene huffed. "Then I spot Kage punching a hole in the wall, not once, but three times."

Jane jerked. "What?"

"I don't think I want to know what made that boy see red, but I also know there's only one person who could make him lose his cool." Charlene held Jane away from her by the shoulders. "Now, I know something is going on in your life and you're keeping it on the down low. I've seen a lot of things in my time, and even though I don't want to know, it wouldn't surprise me a bit if you'd got yourself in a whole heap of trouble."

Garrett growled. "Charlene—"

"Don't Charlene me, boy. I watched you lose your momma to cancer, your dad to a heart attack, and spanked your butt myself when you needed to be set back on the right path. That means I have a right to say whatever I want, and I got something to say." Charlene inhaled and narrowed her eyes. "I can see in Janie's demeanor she's gone through a rough spot. Anyone looking at her can tell she's doing her best to outrun trouble. She has you and those other two out there trying to talk Kage down so he doesn't hurt himself or someone else. But Kage hasn't had one damn good thing in his life, and he's the one I'm concerned about right now. I was around when Kage's family crumbled, and I know what his uncle is capable of doing to him. I've seen it with my own two eyes. A man gets desperate and stupid when his woman is threatened."

"Shit," Garrett muttered before exiting the room.

Charlene turned back to Jane, her eyes softening but her hold never relaxing. "You don't know it, but you're the only thing holding that boy from walking away from everything he's built. For some reason, in a world of devastation, he only sees you."

Jane shook her head, not understanding the direction Charlene was taking the conversation. Kage was the strongest person she knew. He was confident, secure, and chose to keep to himself. It was surprising he even became friends with Garrett and the others, because he needed no one.

She stood. "He only wants to have sex with me."

A rude sound came from Charlene's lips. "That boy could have sex with anyone he wants but he's not, because he wants you."

A strange sensation fluttered around her heart. Charlene was right. Kage never brought anyone into his life. She'd heard the talk, listened in on Garrett's conversations enough in the past to know that Kage had plenty of women, but he'd never once brought one home or around the others.

Jane pinched the skin at the base of her neck. "It's only because I need his protection."

"You're making excuses," Charlene stated. "You know deep in your heart that something big is going on between you two. It's always been there, any fool can see it."

He'd held her, protected her, kissed her. And not any kind of kiss, but a kiss that promised so much more.

"I can't do this," she whispered. "I'm not the woman for him."

"What are you talking about?" Charlene snapped.

"You don't know what I've been through," she said. "No one does."

Charlene rounded on her and got in her face. "No, I don't. And I can't even tell you what Kage's gone through either, but I've lived long enough to know that boy's haunted. A lesser man would've given up and admitted defeat. Not Kage. He fights, and he walks through a world that hasn't been kind to him, because he's in love with you."

Jane's head came up.

"That's right. I don't even know if Kage realizes it, but I've watched you two since you were kids. He latched onto you, soaking up all the goodness and kindness you'd give him. Then you came back, and all I see is you pushing him away, feeling sorry for yourself." Charlene sank down on her knees in front of Jane. "You're so afraid of someone hurting you; you don't see that you're hurting everyone around you."

Jane's stomach cramped. "You don't know what could happen if—"

"No, I don't. But shutting Kage out isn't going to help. You're stronger than you think you are, and so is he." Charlene stood, walked to the door, and hesitated. "The Janie I knew had a smart mouth and would throw herself into the middle of a fight to save the underdog. You often got in trouble because you were determined to spread your wings before you were ready, but you were never a bitch."

Charlene left much more quietly than she'd arrived. Jane didn't want to be a bitch, but no one knew what she'd gone through. How many times did she have to tell them before they got it?

She wrinkled her nose. Shit.

She was pathetic. Not only had she allowed Scott to strip her of all self-respect, she'd continued to drown herself in her problems instead of fighting back. Charlene was right. She had the chance to turn her life around when she got back, and to forget about Scott for good. Yet she continued living in the past.

Instead of fighting, she'd let others fight for her and hurt everyone in the end. She was going to put an end to pathetic Jane and start acting like Janie. She gasped. That's what Kage meant all along.

She cupped her elbows in her hands. How could Charlene tell that Kage was haunted?

He'd always been quiet, preferring to spend time with himself rather than with everyone in town. The times he did go out, he was always with the boys. She remembered the piece of paper he'd given her. Her heart warmed, and instantly the warmth turned into pain.

She'd been so caught up in her life, she'd missed the significance of him stepping out to help her. He'd offered himself to her. Whether that was for safety, help, or more, she'd shrugged him off.

Yet, on her return, he was still the first to go to battle for her. She covered her face. He'd even told her when she'd questioned why he kissed her. It was right in front of her face, and she couldn't see anything because she'd let Scott dictate her life.

A loud crash came from somewhere in the building. She rushed to the door and ran out into the hallway as Kage body-slammed Tony against the wall.

Kage caught her eye. His dark gaze, panicked and raw with emotions, held onto her, soaking her in. She stared back, letting him see that she was okay, assuring him that she was there for him.

He stepped toward her, but Lance planted his hands on Kage's chest. He jolted away from the touch. His mouth opened as if he wanted to speak to her, but he changed his mind. Never had she seen Kage out of control. It made his scary tough attitude seem like a Sunday afternoon.

"Check yourself." Lance strained. "Calm down!"

The whole time Kage's gaze was locked on Jane. She retreated. It was true that she'd messed everything up, but she was going to make things right.

"Get the fuck out of my space." Kage's eyes were on her, but his words were aimed at Lance.

She stayed in the hallway, only because her legs shook and she doubted she could walk away without falling. "Lance, let him go," she said, more calmly than she was feeling.

Lance glanced behind him. "Jane, give him a moment."

"No." She stepped forward and laid her hand on Lance's back. "He won't hurt me."

"I have a stomach that says differently," Lance said.

Kage shoved him out of the way. Then he was in front of her, breathing hard, staring down in her eyes. She swallowed. The truth of what Charlene had told her was right in front of her.

He grabbed her hand, pulling her into the holding room, and slammed the door. She stood, waiting for him to explain what was going on. To explain to her why he fought so hard and refused to back away when she'd given him every reason to want her gone.

Instead, he stepped toward her, framed her face with his hands, and used his thumbs to raise her chin. "Whatever happens, whatever you hear, I want you to remember what I'm going to tell you."

She nodded.

"Tomorrow, I'll get a phone call and I will leave. I shouldn't be gone long, but I want you to stick with the guys. Listen to what they tell you, and make sure you're never alone. Don't give them any lip or think you can go out by yourself. I need your word. Can you do that for me?"

"Where are you going?"

He blew out his breath, pulled her to his chest, and wrapped his arms around her. "To stop Carson."

"No." She jerked, but he pressed her head against his chest.

"Do you trust me?" He left no room for her to argue.

"Yes, but I don't trust Scott." She held on to him tighter. "Don't go. Stay here with me."

His body hardened and his hand shook against her head. "You're going to have to trust me, baby."

She slipped from his embrace. She had to make sure he understood. "I do. I've always trusted you, Kage."

He reached for her, and she spotted his hand. "Oh my God."

Cut and bleeding, his hand already showed signs of swelling over the angry rawness marking his knuckles. She grabbed his wrist, pulled him toward the bed, and pushed him down, amazed when he allowed her to command him.

"Stay right there." She wagged her finger at him. "I'm going to the control room to get some things to clean you up."

She jogged into the headquarters. "I need a first aid kit."

Tony's brows rose. "He's going to let you help him?"

"I gave him no choice," she said.

"Kage always has a choice, darling." Tony keyed into the computer.

Ignoring Tony's remark, she looked to Lance. "Do you know where I can find one?"

"Yeah. I'll get it for you." Lance left the room.

She followed him down the hall. He handed her a small box but held on to it.

"What?" she said.

His eyes softened. "Don't hurt him."

"I'm trying to make his hand feel better, not worse." She tugged at the box, but he still refused to hand it over.

"I'm not talking about his hand, Janie," he whispered.

She sucked in her breath. Did everyone know what went through Kage's head but her? "I won't."

He grinned, letting her take the first aid kit. She whirled around and hurried back to the room.

Without saying a word, she kneeled in front of Kage and cleaned his wounds. She was occupied with the task, but her mind was on the man. After the last butterfly strip was in place, she held his palm and kissed each knuckle. Kage used his other hand to stroke the back of her head, and she leaned into his touch.

She raised her gaze. "I'm going with you."

He gave his head a shake. "No."

Now that she'd spoken, she gained confidence. A piece of her that'd gone missing four years ago returned with a familiar strength. She spread her hands out on his stomach, anchoring herself to him. Solid, strong, and brave, he needed to believe how much she needed him in her life. This had nothing to do with Scott but with them. "I'm the only one who can get Scott out of hiding, but I won't feel protected without you there with me. You and *only* you can do this. You'll keep me safe, and together we'll make everything right."

She only hoped he would still want her when all of this was over.

Chapter Eleven

A half hour later, Kage grinned at the way Jane fussed over him. He'd waited for her to gain back the confidence Scott stole from her, and once she made her mind up to do whatever needed to be done to put Scott behind her, she went pedal to the metal. Not only did she stand up for him, showing her belief that he could keep her safe, but all the guys from the agency gave her moral support and seemed to enjoy watching him squirm under her attention.

"So, you'll let me help if anything happens, right?" she asked everyone in the room but looked only at Kage.

"Janie…" He gazed up at the ceiling before directing his attention back to her. He knew he'd give in. She was the one person he had a hard time saying no to. "Fine. But you have to listen to me at all times."

"Absolutely." She lunged at him, throwing her arms around his waist.

"I think we can go home now." Kage ducked his head and spoke into her ear, so the other guys wouldn't overhear. "Alone."

"Good. I'm ready." Jane leaned against him and whispered, "I can't wait."

He cut off the growl that crept inside his throat and backed her toward the wall. "You have no idea how much you're turning me on right now or how long I've waited to hear you say those words."

"Yeah?" Her lips softened, her gaze meeting his as she laid her hands on his stomach. "I could keep talking if you want me to."

"What?" His hands went to the wall, and he pressed into her, blocking her escape.

"I have a lot to say. Like how I love how you refuse to let me pull back from you, because it gives me an excuse to follow my heart, and have I mentioned how when you walk across the room, everyone stops what they're doing and stares…including me?" She ran her hands over his chest and looped her arms around his neck. "How hot I get when you—"

"Janie…" His body flashed hot and he leaned down, hovering his mouth over her lips. "Damn, baby."

She inched forward. "Kage?"

He kissed her softly. "You get it."

"I get it," she said, against his lips.

Shoving off the wall, he grabbed her hand and led her across the room. She uttered no protest, and he liked that she wasn't fighting what was happening between them any longer.

"Hey, where are you two going?" Garrett asked.

He opened the door, and without breaking stride, said, "Home."

At the car, he set her inside, buckled her seat belt, and hesitated to leave her. Adrenaline made him shaky, and he wished they were already home. Even though he lived on the outskirts of town and the drive only took ten minutes, the distance it took to drive home would keep him from touching her, and he wanted all her attention right now.

She shivered and blinked. He glanced down at her breasts. Her nipples were hard and showing through her shirt. Oh yeah, she was ready. There was no doubt in his mind that today's events had her highly attuned to him and they were thinking the same thing. He crouched outside the passenger door, needing her close. For the first time since he was a kid, he was unsure if he was doing everything right. He wasn't the type of guy to romance a chick or spend time bullshitting his way into her bed. He wanted to assure her that he'd never hurt her and his feelings for her couldn't be stronger. Most of all, he wanted to do everything perfectly for her.

Janie's show of support meant the world to him. He'd had no one, cared about no one, and yet when it came to her, he wanted and needed her. If he had the words, he'd tell her exactly how she was his reason for breathing. But he feared even that wouldn't match the emotions overflowing inside of him.

Instead, he said, "Thank you."

She gazed at his lips, her own breaking into a tender smile that wrapped around his heart and warmed him. "Take me home, honey."

He'd told her she'd have to come to him, hoping she'd understand what he'd been telling her. After calling his uncle, he'd thought walking away from his need to have her would be in Jane's best interest. But in the end, she made the first move.

He could see it in her eyes. The way she'd touched him, the things she'd said. The little hitch in her voice when she spoke was his undoing. She teetered on the edge of something big, and he was selfish enough, he wouldn't let her slip away.

He grinned, feeling damn good. He gave her one more solid kiss, closed the door, and quickly surveyed the area before loping around the front of the car.

As he turned around in the parking lot, he caught sight of Garrett standing by the back door. He lifted his chin. Garrett's penetrating gaze followed the car, but before losing sight of him, Kage received a chin lift in return.

He held her hand all the way home, disengaging only to shift gears. He pulled into his driveway and set the emergency brake.

He killed the engine.

Hyperaware that he had to stay focused on her safety, he walked her to the front door of the house, shutting off the alarm and resetting it once they were inside. Then he turned to her. His breath came fast and hard.

"Come here." He stood with his arms loose at his side.

She took one, two, three steps, until she stood in front of him, neither of them touching. Then she leaped and he caught her. His hands went to her ass. Her arms went around his neck, and he carried her to the bedroom without taking his mouth off her.

In the bedroom, he slid her down his body, enjoying the mixed pleasure and pain of her soft flesh rubbing against his hard one. He took the end of her shirt and pulled it over her head, sucking in his breath.

The denim bra barely covered the bottom half of her breasts. He trailed his finger over the top of each mound, watching her chest rise as she inhaled swiftly.

"Kage?"

Buff meowed her hello from her spot on the bed.

"I've waited so long for this," he murmured. "So sweet."

He stripped off his own shirt and then moved to her jeans. The belt came undone, and he yanked it out of the loops and tossed it across the room. Bluff meowed in a huff at the interruption and ran out the door.

Jane put her hand on her zipper, blocking Kage from taking off her jeans "Wait."

"Baby..."

"I need to—" She leaned forward and rested her forehead on his chest. "Oh, God."

He tangled his fingers in the hair at the back of her head and brought her face toward him. "What do you need?"

She squeezed her eyes shut, opened them, and said, "Only you."

"You got me." He captured her lips.

Nothing else mattered.

He made quick work of removing her clothes. The rest of his—jeans, boxers, and boots—came off next. The whole time, he kept her at his side, until he was sure there would be nothing separating them. Then he backed her onto the bed, landed on top of her, and braced his weight on his arms.

"I need to taste you, baby." He kissed his way down her body, taking his time.

He licked the warm pulse at her neck then left light kisses along her collarbone. He wanted to dive straight to her breasts, but he forced himself to wait. He'd gone this long imagining how she'd taste, he wanted to savor the moment and enjoy every inch.

Jane arched against him, and he pulled back and gazed down on her. "So fucking beautiful."

He lowered his head, took her nipple into his mouth, and sucked. His eyes closed voluntarily. She was perfect in every way. He teased her with his tongue, eliciting a moan from Jane. With his hand, he cupped the slope of her breasts.

"Kage…" Jane sank her hands into his hair.

He raised his gaze and moved down her body over her breasts, her nipples, her stomach, and gazed up at her as he settled between her legs. He'd fantasized about this moment for years. Every detail he imagined paled with reality.

"Kage, I've never had someone do this…You can't." She wrinkled her nose, squirming against the hold he had on her hips.

He lowered his head to her sex.

"Oh. My. God." She moaned.

He smiled against her, showing her exactly what she could expect each and every time with him. He'd do this all day long and never get tired of tasting, feeling, experiencing her pleasure against his mouth.

Jane writhed underneath him. Her hands came to his hair, and her upper body leaped off the bed. He continued, a lick here. A nip there. Until he gave her what she cried for and zeroed in, taking her all the way.

She moaned his name as her thighs clenched around his head, trembling with the power of her orgasm. He slowed, bringing her down softly. Her body jolted with each swipe of his tongue.

She inhaled a shuddering breath and collapsed, arms thrown out to the side. He crawled up on the bed, stretched over her to open the nightstand drawer. She watched him remove a condom and put it on before settling back between her legs.

"Open your eyes." He kissed the curve of her jaw. "I want to watch you as I make you come again."

"Twice?" Her eyes flashed open. "I can't…I've never…"

"I like hearing you say that." He hardened even more, and his balls grew tight. "And you will. Give it to me and only me. You're mine, baby, only mine."

She ran her hands up his arms, over his shoulders, and something happened in her face he'd never seen before. She softened. Her lips parted, her eyes grew glossy, and her eyelids struggled to stay open. He moved his hips, barely touching his cock to the entrance to her pussy when her eyelids fluttered again.

He groaned and plunged into her wetness. She gasped as he moved ever so slowly. In and out. His body tightened and he fought to keep control. His cock hardened to a level he'd never experienced when her leg curled around his hip. So fucking tight, she sucked him in and he never wanted to leave.

"Yes, yes." She arched her neck.

He stilled. "Look at me."

She clawed his shoulders and eased her head back. Eyelashes fluttered. He grinned, waiting. When she connected and melted underneath him, he drove into her.

In.

Out.

In.

Out.

He didn't miss a stroke. "Eyes on me."

She fought to keep her eyes open. His toes curled. God, that was sexy. Having her zoned in on what they were doing, him being the center of her universe, there was nothing better.

He slipped his hand between her body and his, found her heat, and slowly rubbed her. Her neck arched, giving him a full view of her that he'd dreamed about every time he closed his eyes.

"That's it, baby. Give it to me."

She panted. Jaw tight, struggling to stay focused on her, he lost control. His body seized in extreme pleasure, rolling through him from head to toe. Her eyelids fluttered. He thrust deep and let her orgasm bring him to release.

Spent, he lowered himself to his elbows, cradling her head in his hands. A full-body sigh swept through him as he caught his breath. She added her own moan of contentment underneath him, and he chuckled in her ear. "Yeah?"

"Yeah," she whispered.

He closed his eyes and enjoyed the way she kept rubbing her hands along his sides. Eventually his arms gave out, and he flipped to his side, taking her with him.

She snuggled against him. "Kage?"

"Hm?"

"I'm going with you. You're not going to change your mind again, right?" she asked, propping herself on her elbow.

He leaned in, until his forehead touched hers. "Right now, you're exactly where I've always wanted you. In my bed, letting me hold you, wrapping your arms around me. I don't want to talk about anything else but you and me. This is our time, baby."

"But I need to—"

The doorbell rang.

He bolted to a sitting position. *Shit.*

"Who's that?" she asked.

"I don't know, but I'm going to find out." He pulled on his jeans from the floor, picked up his pistol off the dresser, and stalked to the door. He hesitated and gazed over his shoulder. "Stay here. I'll be right back."

Chapter Twelve

Rushing to find her clothes, Jane strained to hear what was happening at the front door. Fear mingled with the contentment she'd found in Kage's arms. She blamed Scott for invading every aspect of her life.

She'd finally had Kage to herself after wanting him since forever, and she wasn't ready to let go of the security he brought her. She shoved her foot into her jeans and hopped into them. *Damn Scott.*

How could she enjoy all the new and old feelings Kage brought out when something always happened to bring her back to reality? She hooked her bra and slipped into her shirt. Maybe it was one of the boys or even a friend of Kage's who'd stopped by to say hey. She knew it couldn't have been Scott because he wasn't the walk-up-and-ring-the-doorbell type.

But maybe that was Scott's plan. To take them by surprise. She rubbed her forehead, looking around for a weapon, and panicked when she could not find one freaking thing to use. She'd wait another minute before going to see what was happening.

The sounds of a scuffle came from the other side of the door, and a loud familiar "Let us in." Charlene burst in with Sabrina. Jane's jaw dropped open.

Sabrina, looking beautiful in a pair of skinny jeans tucked into a pair of sexy black boots with four-inch heels, a gypsy blouse that flowed around her lean frame, topped with a rich-looking scarf that hung to her knees, stared back at her. Both screamed at the same time. Sabrina launched herself at Jane as Jane dove for Sabrina.

They collided, laughing on the bed in a tangle of sheets. She hugged Sabrina tight, not wanting to let her go again. Time simply didn't exist now that she'd seen her best friend.

"Charlene told me you were home. Then she told me you were with Kage." Sabrina pulled back. "Holy shit, girl. You're with *Kage*." Her eyes grew round. "I can't believe—I am sitting in Kage Archer's bed."

Jane cringed but Sabrina laughed.

It was one thing to share her secret of sleeping with Kage in private and have a girlish giggle while spilling every delicious detail with her best friend, but Kage was watching her. She exhaled on a quiver. The turn of events gave her bragging rights, because he was way better in bed than she and Sabrina had ever imagined.

Honest and genuine, Sabrina always told her exactly what she was thinking. It was the reason Jane loved her best friend and why she'd made the decision to distance herself while she was with Scott. If no one knew what she was living through, then she could pretend her life didn't suck.

She glanced at the door. Kage leaned against the door frame. a half grin on his face, looking mighty pleased with himself. His gaze was on her. though, and she realized he always seemed centered on her no matter where they were. She warmed. Moments ago they'd had sex in this very same bed.

She freaked, pulling Sabrina off the sheets. "Get up. Get up."

"What?" Sabrina looked between her and Kage, and Jane knew

the moment Sabrina figured out what was going on before she walked in. "Oh, no. There is no way you're keeping this to yourself. I want to hear exactly how you managed to have the elusive Kage Archer nail you in his own freaking bed, in his own freaking house. I think this is a first. Maybe I should look for a knife, and you can put the notch in his headboard because Kage has declared you his woman. I love it."

"Sh!" Jane tugged Sabrina to her, embarrassed yet thrilled to have her friend there to share this with. She'd missed her dearly. "We're—"

Kage knocked lightly on the door to get their attention, still grinning but looking at only her. "I'll be in the kitchen." His gaze locked on her body. "Baby, take your time with your friends, and I'll put on some coffee for everyone."

Charlene cackled and slapped Kage on the back. "I don't think it's coffee that girl needs. She needs food to keep up with you. You can't be wearing her out when she's under so much stress."

Jane couldn't be embarrassed. It was Kage. He'd fascinated her since she'd been a teen, and now she'd had sex with him. Wonderful, mind-blowing sex. The likes of which she'd never had before. Ever.

"Are you hungry, baby?" Kage studied her. "It's dinnertime."

Oh. My. God. Her insides went mushy, and she nodded. Kage gave her a knowing, satisfied grin before heading in the direction of the kitchen. She knew what he was thinking and couldn't help teasing him as she replied, "Starving."

"Geez, turn on the air conditioner, you two." Sabrina waved her hand in front of her face.

"I'll help Kage. Lord knows, that man shouldn't be using his beautiful muscles to cook. He should stand somewhere, so we women can gaze at him whenever we want. Mm-hm." Charlene left the room.

Sabrina turned to Jane, eyes filled with tears. "I've missed you so much, and now Charlene tells me something bad is happening and you're involved. What's going on? I thought you were happy living in Pullman."

Jane inhaled deeply, ready to tell her friends the truth. "Let me do something with my hair, brush my teeth, and I'll try to explain."

"You're not in trouble, are you?"

She wrinkled her nose. "Yeah, I got myself into a huge mess, and now Scott—who turned out to be a really, really bad guy—is after me."

"Oh, sweetie." Sabrina gave her one more hug. "I'll help you. Just tell me what I need to do." Jane leaned into her friend. Those words brought her more comfort than she could've imagined. She should have known Sabrina would accept her, problems and all. "Thanks. Now get outta here, before I start crying. You can help Charlene and Kage with breakfast. I'm starving. I'll fill you in on what's happening while we eat."

Ten minutes later, she'd put makeup on, slipped her shoes onto her feet, and walked into the kitchen to find Charlene standing over a waffle maker and the smell of maple syrup in the air. Kage sat at the table, an empty plate in front of him, holding a cup of coffee. She swallowed as he turned to her, unsure if what happened between them changed anything.

His gaze went from questioning to heated as he settled on her. Whoa.

"Sit down, girl. Dinner is ready." Charlene waved the spatula in the air.

"Waffles?" She raised her brows and sat between Kage and Sabrina.

Sabrina leaned closer. "Don't ask. She already yelled at me when I told her no one has waffles at night, unless they want to gain ten pounds."

"I heard that, and you could afford to put on some weight. Men like curves." Charlene slid a plate loaded with waffles, two eggs, and a couple precooked sausages in front of Jane. "Eat. You need to keep up your strength if Kage is going to keep you busy."

Kage coughed on a swallow of coffee. Jane laughed. God, it was good to be back with friends, putting up with their normal outlandish behavior and forgetting what was going on outside in the world. She'd missed this.

"So, spill, chica. Why are you back and what did you do?" Sabrina leaned against the table.

"She ain't going to talk about it. I've tried for the last three weeks and her and Kage's lips are sealed tighter than my blue blouse with the sequins across the shoulders." Charlene harrumphed.

Jane finished chewing and glanced at Kage. He reached out and placed his hand on her thigh, giving her a squeeze. She blew out her breath and leaned back, forgetting about the food.

"Things weren't as great with Scott as I pretended," she said.

Sabrina frowned and Charlene fell silent behind her. She continued. "It was bad." She glanced at Kage. "I sorta stole Scott's gun and some of his money when I ran away."

"Wait. Back up the truck." Sabrina waved her hand. "Bad? How bad?"

Kage straightened and spoke to Jane. "You don't have to—"

"It's okay." She slipped her fingers into his hand. "No more hiding."

"I am not liking the sound of this," Charlene said, her voice low and angry. "No one hurts my girl. Where is this loser now?"

Jane shook her head. "We don't know. That's why I'm staying with Kage. Scott's going to come after me. He always does."

Charlene strode over to Jane, fell to her knees, and gazed up at her in the chair. "What did that rat bastard do?"

"Charlene…" Kage growled.

"Butt out, Kage." Charlene's mouth tightened. "Tell Charlene what happened, so you can heal."

"I'm going outside." Kage shook his head.

Jane watched him exit through the back door. Her stomach rose in her throat, and she swallowed it down. Goose bumps broke out on her arms. She was finally accepting that she wasn't alone. She had Kage, her brother, the guys, Charlene, and Sabrina. So, she told them the story of what'd happened during her relationship with Scott.

She glossed over the times Scott forced himself on her. She also skipped all the times Scott purposely punished her for running away by making a scene in front of the goons who worked for him, for the sake of making himself look good.

She continued summarizing her life with Scott to her friends. "I stole his gun, some of his money, and threw a bag of my clothes and Bluff in the car. Then I drove through five states to come back here. I knew he'd look for me in Bay City, but I needed to buy some time. I figured I'd have a minute to figure out a plan by the time he arrived." She inhaled deeply. "But it'll be over soon. I'm going with Kage and we're going to stop Scott."

As Jane finished, the door opened, allowing a sliver of light to come through. A muttered "Fuck" came from the other side followed by a definite *click*.

Jane frowned, wondering what had upset Kage and why he didn't come back inside.

"Ooh wee, girl. You got right under Kage's skin." Charlene sat down in the empty chair. "Now tell Charlene what you mean by going with him to take down this loser who dared strike my girl."

"I don't know what he plans to do. Kage's not telling me the details. He thinks I'm going to stay here." She splayed her hands on the top of the table. "Yesterday I would've stayed without any questions, but now everything's changed."

"What changed?" Sabrina squeezed her arm. "Are you really in danger?"

She nodded. "Scott's dangerous. He's into a lot of illegal shit and has plenty of men who are eager to do whatever he says."

"I don't like the sound of this." Sabrina frowned. "It kills me to know he hurt you. If I knew where to find him, I'd kick him in the balls. Then when he's hurting, I'd grab his ears and pull his head down into my knee. I'd have to wear my old jeans though 'cause it'd split his nose wide open."

Jane smiled at this coming from someone she knew who screamed when a spider crossed her path. Then she said, "If he shows up, I don't want you anywhere around him. I'm serious, Sab. If I hear you even looked at him, I'll stop being your friend."

Sabrina shrugged and lowered her gaze to the table. "You stopped being my friend when you took up lying to me. Four years of lies, and worst of all, you didn't trust me to help you."

"I *do* trust you!" Jane exclaimed, then lowered her voice. "God, you don't know what it was like."

"Obviously." Sabrina picked apart the paper napkin in front of her. "You were my best friend. It's my job to support you. It was my—"

"I know! I know…" Jane sighed. "I was embarrassed. I lost myself, Sab. I'm still floundering, but a lot has happened the last few days. I'm sick at how I've acted. I was always strong and never let anyone tell me what to do. Then it was like Scott killed that part of me, but I'm finding strength again. I need to make him pay for what he's done."

Sabrina sniffed. "I just feel so damn helpless and mad. You of all people should never be treated that way, especially by a man who doesn't deserve to even breathe the same air as you."

"No one should," Charlene said softly.

"You're really going to go with Kage?" Sabrina asked.

Jane nodded. "Yeah."

"Now that Kage finally has you in his life, he's not going to let you go…or take two feet away from you. He's got it hard for you. Always has." Charlene studied her for a few long seconds until a smile grew on her face. "Makes my heart glad to see two of my favorite people on the way to getting their happily-ever-after. Now, let's hear how good the sex was with him."

"What?" Jane said.

"Sex. The most beautiful thing in the world." Charlene cackled. "It sure isn't my waffles putting a smile on that man's face."

"Charlene!" Jane laughed.

"That's what I'm talking about. Mm-hm." Charlene raised her brows, squinted at Jane and Sabrina, and nodded with experience.

"Today keeps getting juicier." Sabrina squealed. "I need details. Is he good?"

Jane nodded, grinning. "The best."

"I knew it." Sabrina fanned her face. "Did you"—she nudged Jane with her shoulder—"you know?"

Her face heated and she snorted. "I'm not telling."

"Come on." Charlene nudged her. "Let those who'll never know the powers of that sexy body live vicariously through you."

Jane scooted back her chair and stood. "Fine. Yes. I did. Twice."

Both women screamed and clapped their hands. Jane shook her head and looked out the kitchen window when the back door opened. She jumped, whirling around.

"Sorry to interrupt and cut your visit short." Kage pointed to Sabrina and Charlene. "Janie and I have a few things to do. I'll walk you both out."

"What?" Jane walked to Kage's side. "They just got here."

Kage put his hand around her waist, slipped his finger through her belt loop, and pulled her close. "Sun's going to go down soon, and I want them in town before it gets dark."

She sagged against him. "I hate this."

He kissed the top of her head. "I know, but it's only for a little while. Stay here while I walk them out."

Jane hugged and kissed Charlene and Sabrina, promising they'd get together soon. She closed the door, ran to the window, and continued to wave to them as they pulled out of the driveway, despite knowing they couldn't see her. *Damn you, Scott. I'll kill you myself for ripping my life away.*

Kage returned to the house, his gaze finding her. Her stomach flip-flopped. Something was wrong.

He dug into his pocket and extracted a red ribbon with two silver hoops dangling at the bottom. "Do you recognize this?"

She jumped to her feet and rushed over to him, bile burning her throat. He held the ribbon toward her, and she crossed her arms. She didn't have to look or touch it to know it was her missing pair of earrings.

"Where did you find them?" She raked her teeth over her bottom lip.

"When I went outside earlier, I found them on the handle of the back door. I didn't want to say anything with Sabrina and Charlene here. They're yours right?" He dropped his arm to his side.

She nodded. "My missing earrings. I could swear I left them in the bathroom. But maybe I took them off at the garage."

Kage shook his head. She swallowed hard. "So, that's that. He's found me. He's come into the house, took my earrings, and thought it would be funny to show me he can get to me anywhere, even when I'm with you."

"This is a good thing." Kage tossed the earrings on the coffee table. "He's getting careless."

She stared at the ribbon. Nowhere was safe. If Scott could break into the house without tripping the alarm, what was he going to do next?

"I'm scared," she said, walking into Kage's arms. "He was here. In your home. That's not right, Kage. I don't like it."

He held her close, cupping her head against his chest. "Don't worry, baby. Carson's stepped over the line. If he wants to play dirty then we'll play."

Chapter Thirteen

An hour later, phones calls made, incident reported, Kage set down the phone and stalked toward Jane, his gaze intent and heated. Her stomach rolled and her body tingled. She backed up until she felt the wall behind her. She needed something to hold herself upright as waves of desire pulsated through her, threatening to sweep her legs out from under her.

She swayed and caught herself. Um. Okay. She was going to have to figure out a way to control her reactions when alone with Kage.

Swaying from dizziness any time he gave her a look that said he could still taste her on his tongue would not do. He hooked her neck, pulling her to him. Inside, she giggled uncontrollably and wondered if he could hear how silly she sounded.

She held on to his shirt. "What are you doing?"

"I'm trying to kiss you," he murmured.

Oh. Kissing was good. Better than excellent.

His thumb massaged the side of her neck. She trembled and leaned into him.

"You like that, baby." His other hand went to her lower back, holding her in place. "I love how you feel against me."

Standing in front of him she felt vulnerable, stripped of any defenses. Her bare foot slid along his boot. He could crush her, not only her toes, but her whole body, her mind, her heart. She struggled to find herself, find balance after coming out of an abusive relationship with one man into a mind-consuming relationship with Kage that left her breathless.

"I thought we were going to kiss," she whispered.

The corner of his mouth lifted and he nodded. Her gaze dropped to his mouth but he made no move toward her.

She moistened her lips and rubbed them together. "When will this kiss happen?"

His cheek twitched. He was losing the battle of hiding his laughter. Impatient, she planted her hands on the front of his chest and pushed him. Her strength no match for his bulk, she shoved him again with no better results.

"Whatever." She ducked and moved around his body.

She made it barely two feet before he snagged her around the waist, hauling her back against his body. She went limp. He didn't play fair.

"Go in the bedroom, get naked, lie on the bed, and then I'll kiss you," he said in her ear.

Her body melted at his words, but her mind wasn't falling for his ordering her around. She jerked against him. No way was she going to let him dictate how and where they were going to have sex.

She'd spent what seemed like a lifetime doing whatever Scott wanted. To the point where she'd lost herself and hated who'd she'd become. She wouldn't allow Kage to make her feel needy, even if inside she craved him more than what she deemed healthy.

"I'm proud of you, Janie," he whispered.

She stilled. "What?"

"Fight me all you want. Tell me to go to hell. Storm out of the room and refuse to let me touch you." He picked her up, and she grabbed onto his neck to keep from falling. "I would never want you to think you don't have a choice."

"Then why didn't you kiss me instead of ordering me to take my clothes off?" She turned his face toward her.

"Because when I'm around you all I can think about is having you again and having you look at me like I put the sunshine in your day." He walked into the bedroom. "Never doubt how I feel about you. I'm not Scott. I'll never hurt you, physically or mentally. If you want me to go slower or faster, all you have to do is talk to me. I want you to learn that it's okay to say no or to put your own needs first. I want you to believe that you're free from all the shit that darkens your past, baby. Can you trust me to protect you?"

"Yes," she said.

He picked her up and sat down on the bed with her in his lap. She stared at a spot on the wall over his shoulder. He made everything sound easy, and she believed him.

She brought her hands up to his face and placed feather-light kisses to his mouth. "I trust you"—she nibbled—"believe in you"—sucked on his bottom lip, pulling back softly—"and will get naked for you."

She squealed in surprise as he took her to the floor. Her hands went to his shirt, pushing the material over his chest, until he ripped the offending fabric off and flung it behind him. She reached for him, but he rocked back on his knees, his hands making quick work of the zipper of her jeans. A thrill went over her at his hurry, and she laughed, loving every minute.

Kage's hand shook with urgency and his gaze locked on hers. "Condoms are in the bedroom."

She groaned. The wait was killing her. "Go. Hurry."

He pushed himself to his feet and jogged out of the room. She smiled into the empty space and wiggled out of the rest of her clothes. If he wanted her naked, she'd get naked.

She'd just lain back down when he returned, holding up the foil package. She reached for the protection, and he stripped out of his jeans. By the time she was finished rolling on the condom, her own hands shook.

"God, I want you. Now." She pulled him down on top of her.

He captured her mouth, sinking between her thighs. She lifted her hips, sighing against his lips as he entered her with a hard thrust.

There was something about the way he took her that struck a chord deep inside of her. It was more than him wanting her. He *needed* her. His presence in her life went further than sex but brought a balance back within her body and mind, healing her soul. The intensity of how much she wanted to connect with him, to know she could depend on him, surprised her.

She orgasmed, and he quickly followed with a grunt, holding himself on his elbows. His hands framed her face. She studied the pleasure on his face, the harsh breath sweeping over her neck, and her own rapid heartbeat and sensitivity to his touch.

It was all so normal and wonderful.

His gaze softened and he kissed her. "I think we broke records there, baby. Fastest sex ever."

A small giggle bubbled forth, and she buried her face in his shoulder to muffle her laughter. He rolled to the side, taking her with him, and she laughed until tears formed in her eyes. The sound carefree and light even to her own ears.

"No. That was the hottest, best sex ever." She propped her head on her hand. "I could get used to this."

"Yeah?" He heaved himself off the floor and held out his hand. "Be good, and I might be able to give you a repeat performance after I get some work done."

She stilled putting on her shirt. "Work?"

"Got some things to check out." He grabbed his clothes and dressed.

"Can't it wait?" she asked.

He shook his head. "Sorry, baby. I'll hurry and then we'll spend the rest of the evening together."

He moved over and kissed her. She grabbed his shirt, holding him in place. His hands gently removed hers before he brought them to his mouth, kissed each palm, and then turned and walked toward the hallway.

"Wait." She shoved her arms in her T-shirt and hurried to follow. "I'll help."

"I got this covered." He brushed the hair out of her eyes. "Give me an hour. Why don't you watch a movie or call Sabrina?"

She grabbed his wrist. "Tell me what you're doing."

"I said I got it covered." He leaned down and laid his lips on her forehead, dismissing her.

"Kage…" She planted her fists on her hips.

"Don't get in a snit—"

"Snit?" she whispered. "You jerk. You promised me you'd let me help."

Her body vibrated with anger. She hated when Kage shut her out of what was going on, especially since it concerned her.

"Baby," he said, reaching for her.

She held out her hand. "Don't come any closer."

He stopped, not saying a word.

"You can't do this." She pulled in a breath, but couldn't seem to gather enough air to fill her lungs. "I won't put up with it."

"Put up with what?" Kage asked.

"That!" She pointed at him. "You placing me in a bubble, telling me I can help but keeping me out of the loop. Now you're going to work on how to find Scott, and because you think I'll crack, you're protecting me. If you're going to leave me, the least you can do is give me back my gun."

"No gun."

"That's not your decision to make, Kage. You're not my boyfriend. I'm not anything to—"

He crossed the room in three strides and held her arms to her sides. "You're everything, don't you know? What do you think it means when I put you in my bed? When I put you in my home? When I go to sleep at night with you by my side?"

She crossed her arms. "I don't know."

"You are the person I want to see before I go to bed, want to wake up to every morning. I love the feel of you in my arms. I've been deep inside your body, tasted you on my tongue, and I'll continue doing the same thing every day until you realize I'm not going anywhere. *You're* not going anywhere." He paused, closing his eyes for a split second before focusing on her. "I know we're going fast, so please tell me if this isn't what you want. Always remember, when you're around me, you can voice your thoughts. You can have an opinion. You have the right to walk away from me."

She frowned. That's not what she wanted, even though he'd made her mad. She liked feeling safe with him more.

His fingers loosened and he rubbed her arms. "That doesn't mean I'll let you walk into danger. When I know more, you'll know. Trust me."

She shook her head. "I don't get this kind of relationship. Everything you do confuses me."

He brought her closer and wrapped his arms around her. "I'm not Carson."

"I know that," she muttered.

"Do you remember me telling you that I was going to call you

Janie until you remembered what it was like before you were scared to be yourself, to rely on other people?"

"It's impossible to forget how much I've changed. It seems easier to believe that person is gone."

"Is she?" He chuckled. "Hell, who was that woman who called me a jerk a second ago?"

Her heart raced. "I fought with you."

"Yeah." He kissed her forehead. "You did."

She stared up at him. "You did it on purpose."

"No, I need to make a phone call. Though I'm glad you're back to standing up for yourself." His gaze heated and he stepped around her. "If I learn anything, I promise you'll be the first to know. If not, you'll have to trust me that I know what's best for you. Afterward, I'll do my best at helping you get over your anger." He smiled that sexy, mischievous smile and she knew exactly what he had in mind.

"You're really not going to let me hear what's going on?"

He paused in the hallway and gazed at her. "You want me to kiss you?"

"Yes," she whispered.

He smiled a full hundred-watt smile. "Then let me get to work, so I can come and find your ass in my bed, baby."

Kage walked away from her without looking back. She caught her bottom lip between her teeth. He was up to something.

He'd held up to his promise and kept her informed on what the boys found out at the agency—which was nothing new. Scott wasn't even the man she was led to believe. She had no idea of his real name or where he came from. It was like he created a whole new life when he'd met her on campus. She'd fallen for his pretty words and smooth moves.

She crept to the entrance of the hallway and peeked down it. The bedroom door was shut, so she tiptoed all the way down and pressed her ear against the door. For several minutes the only thing she heard was silence in the room. Then Kage's voice drifted to her.

"I'm calling in a favor," he said.

She raised her hands and laid her palms on the wood. Her heart raced, making it hard to hear.

"Right." He paused. "No, nobody knows I've talked with you, and I'll be coming alone."

She pulled away and walked back to the living room. Determined not to let Kage know she overheard part of his conversation, she pulled the pans out of the cabinet and slammed them on the counter. If he thought he'd sneak away and deal with Scott by himself, he was crazy. She wasn't going to let him leave her sight.

Chapter Fourteen

The sound of Kage's cell phone ringing broke him out of his sleep. Jane lay asleep on his arm, and he reached over with his other hand to snag the phone off the nightstand without waking her. He came wide awake at seeing the blocked sender alert.

"Yeah?" he said.

"One hour. 1746 Elm Street. Back door's open." *Click.*

His muscles tightened. He'd expected to travel to meet Darrell, not have him show up in Bay City. He tossed the phone, rolled toward Jane, and kissed her softly. "Wake up, baby."

She squirmed deeper against him. His body hardened at the warmth radiating off her, and he pushed the idea of staying home and enjoying her out of his mind. The meeting with Darrell hopefully meant an end to Jane's nightmare.

He pulled the blanket off them and sat up. "Come on, we have to go."

"Sleepy," she mumbled, turning to her stomach.

He crossed the room in the dark and turned on the lights. The sun wasn't even up yet. He knew his uncle would create a meeting to his advantage. What Darrell didn't know was that Kage had expected no warning—the odd hour notice, and the secretive nature of the meeting—and had prepared ahead of time. He was ready.

After using the bathroom, he slipped on his jeans and shirt, fastened his boots, and glanced at the bed. Jane, naked and uncovered, continued to sleep. Her round, firm ass tempted him to undress.

He gave her a soft yet startling slap on the very part of her body that teased him. "If you're planning on going with me, you better get up. I've got business going down."

She jolted awake. "Now?"

"Yes, now. Get a move on. You've got ten minutes to get dressed, or I'm calling the guys in to stay at the house with you." He watched understanding sweep over her features, and he schooled his reaction. If Carson could see her now, he would be worried. His girl was out for blood.

He was proud of her for staying strong. Scott hadn't been able to break her spirit the way Kage had feared. It made him more determined to see this meeting through. She trusted and believed in him, and he wouldn't disappoint her.

She scrambled out of the bed. "I'm ready."

"Ten minutes." He walked out of the room, slipping his holster into the holder at his ribs.

If yesterday and last night had taught him anything, he knew better than to leave her alone in the house, even with one of the guys to protect her. Her confidence and drive to stand up for herself was coming back fast. A full-on Janie with attitude was not something he wanted to deal with today on top of the meeting.

She'd walk all over Lance and Tony. All she had to do was soften her voice, and Garrett catered to her every wish. Kage would have to handle her himself. The fact that she cared enough about him she was willing to put herself in danger warmed him and made him more determined to keep her out of trouble.

In the spare room, he opened the closet and removed the blanket covering the gun safe. He used his keys to unlock the door and removed a .380 and a buck knife, shoving two full clips into his back pocket. He raised his pant leg, put the pistol in the top of his boot, and slid the knife into the two-inch cutout on the outside of his ankle sheath. His jeans hid the handle from view.

Kage stood and paused before closing the safe. His gaze went to the left side of the hutch where he'd stored his father's weapons. His uncle had presented them to him when he was twenty-one, and along with the family heirlooms of guns, safes, and weaponry used in the drug trade, his uncle had offered him a job in the family business. He shut the door, locked the safe, and left the room.

Digging through the past raised questions he refused to look at right now. What caused his uncle to turn his back on his own blood? What sort of pleasure put money over doing the right and decent thing? How could he live with himself after all the things he had done?

His uncle was powerful enough to ruin Kage's life with a snap of his fingers. Kage needed to focus on one thing at a time. First came Jane's safety.

Jane hopped on one foot, pulling her boot on. He waited in the hallway, watching her. She should never have to live wondering if her life was in danger or always looking behind her, afraid her world would turn bad.

She grabbed her purse off the dresser. "I'm ready."

He couldn't help grinning. She'd put on a pair of black jeans and a black long-sleeve T-shirt, and pulled her hair back into a ponytail. Her effort to prove she was ready to take out Scott and not get caught was cute. The electric pink *DIVA* scrolled across her shirt announced to anyone who saw her of her amateur sniper status.

"We'll walk outside the same way we always do." He caught himself ogling her breasts and looked away. "Stay at my side and be quiet. It's dark out."

She walked with him to the front room. "What time is it?"

"Three." He removed his phone.

"In the morning?" She shook her head and snorted. "I'm going to look like shit later."

"You're always beautiful." He kissed her softly. "Hang on a second. I need to call headquarters."

The phone rang once in his ear before Tony answered. "Yo."

"Hey. I'm moving." Kage switched the phone to his other ear and turned his face away from Jane. "I've got company coming in with me."

"Bro…tell me she did not talk you into taking her."

He keyed off the alarm on the door. "No. We'll be at the garage in fifteen. Notify the others."

"Sonofabitch." Tony groaned. "It's too early to deal with her."

Kage glanced at Jane, applying lipstick, a little round mirror held out in front of her. Fierceness to protect her came over him. He would not allow anyone to take her away from him again.

"I'm out." He disconnected the call, knowing Tony would have everything ready when they arrived.

Kage moved toward Jane, wanting to tell her how much he admired her, and instead he kissed her. She gasped in pleasure, and he used the opportunity to taste her. He pulled away gently with soft kisses, gazing into her eyes.

"Ready?" he said.

"Yeah." She moved to the couch, picked up Bluff, whispered in the cat's ear before putting her back on the pillow, and returned to him. She nodded. "Let's get him."

Kage fought a grin and opened the door. With Jane tucked to his side, his hands free, he surveyed the yard on the way to his car.

He wouldn't put it past his uncle to have men watching his every move, on top of worrying about Scott out there somewhere, biding his time to get Jane alone.

Halfway to town, he caught Jane watching him. "What?"

"You're serious," she said.

"This is serious business." He flipped on his signal, slowed down, and turned onto the main road leading into town.

"What exactly are we doing?"

He was meeting the man he hated more than anyone in the world, breaking all the rules he'd made for himself life. And he would end up owing his life to his uncle, all to save Jane's. Letting the thought drop, he said, "A meeting with someone who can make Scott disappear from your life."

"Shit," she whispered. "You mean kill him or send him to Siberia, right?"

"Not my decision." He shifted down. "I need to stop in at headquarters first."

Jane fell silent. He turned into the parking lot, went directly behind the garage, and parked in front of the agency door. Tony's Camaro and Lance's Harley were both in the lot. Garrett probably walked over from the house the moment he got the call.

Before he could open his door and tell Jane to wait, she grabbed his arm. "This could be dangerous, huh?"

He nodded.

"Then maybe I need a gun. You know, so I can have your back," she said.

He kissed her hard and fast. "No gun."

"What if something happens to you? I could be your only hope of getting out of there safely," she protested before flopping back onto her seat.

He glanced at the clock on the dash and exited the vehicle. Time was running out. No one made his uncle wait without paying for the inconvenience later, including him. He could handle whatever Darrell dished out, but he had Jane to think about now.

"Come on, baby." He held out his hand and kept her by his side as they moved to the agency door.

Lance opened the door. Kage nodded and led Jane down the hallway. Out the corner of his eye, he saw Garrett and Tony come out of headquarters and follow him.

"I thought you had to go to the office?" Jane stopped and turned toward him.

She missed Lance slipping behind her and opening the door on the left. Kage backed Jane into the room. "I'll explain later."

Her gaze darted around the vacant holding room. "What are you doing?"

"Keeping you safe." He took two steps backward. "I'll be back."

She looked behind him. "Garrett. Don't let him—"

He shut the door and faced Garrett. "Do not let her out or I'll come after you."

"Hey!" She banged on the door. "Let me out of here. Kage! Don't do this!"

Tony caught Kage's gaze. "Need backup?"

He shook his head. "Stay here. I want all of you on guard. Don't let her talk you into letting her out of your sight. Carson gets ahold of her, he's not going to let her escape this time."

"Lance put a tracer on the Mustang." Garrett clapped him on the shoulder. "Don't argue, or I'll follow you underground."

Relief swept through him. Despite his bravery, knowing they knew his location if something happened made him feel better. "Thanks."

"Stay focused." Garrett walked with him a few feet. "You better act fast, and get your ass back here. We've got your back from this end, so concentrate on getting the information you need. From this side, nobody will know if you keep low and stay out of trouble."

"Just watch out for Janie," Kage said.

Without waiting for a reply, he strode to the exit. It was time to meet his uncle and handle business. He pushed Jane out of his mind. He had to stay focused, get the job done, and come back to the guys and Jane with his name clean. Hopefully, Jane would forgive him for leaving her and realize it was his only choice. He couldn't put her in further danger.

Chapter Fifteen

Jane couldn't believe Kage left her. She fisted her hands at her sides to keep from hitting something. He'd led her to believe he was okay with her helping, and then he dropped her off without a second thought.

What if he got hurt? Who would be there to help him? What if he died and never came back?

Jane kicked the door again and a jolt of pain traveled through her big toe. She grimaced and limped to the bed against the far wall. He was supposed to take her to the mysterious meeting, so she'd have a hand in what happened to Scott.

It was her fight, not his. She grabbed the chair, tried to heave it, and cried out in pain when it didn't move an inch. "Real freaking stupid, you dumbasses," she screamed. "Let me out of here. Kage needs me."

"Sis?" Garrett's voice filled the room. "Calm down. You're in the holding room for a reason. It's the safest place you can be right now."

"No shit, Sherlock." She searched the ceiling, the walls, looking for the intercom. "Unlock the door now or I swear, when I get out of here—"

"It's for your own good," Garrett said.

"I can't believe this." She fisted her hands on her hips. "Since when do you listen to Kage? Hm? Aren't you the boss?"

Garrett cussed. "Not anymore. We've partnered on the agency end of business."

That was news to her, although not surprising. Dad had given her a quarter share in Beaumont Body Shop years ago, but Garrett had taken the agency in a higher direction during her absence.

"Please, Garrett. I can't stand to be in here." She peered up at the corner of the room. "Will you let me out if I promise to hang with you? I won't even talk or bother you."

Several seconds passed. "We'll let you out when Kage returns. It's early. Why don't you take a nap?"

She grabbed her purse and searched the contents. "This is exactly why I should have a gun. I'd shoot my way out, and then I'd hit each one of you pathetic excuses for a man over the head with it. How you guys can be so good looking and egotistically conceited is beyond me. If I ever get out of here and get my life back, I'm buying a billboard warning all women to stay away from the Beaumont Body Shop."

Their laughter that had carried into the room quickly ended on her last threat. She threw her purse against the wall in frustration. There was nothing in it that she could use as a tool to pry open the door. The minute she got out of here, she was stealing one of their pistols, *and* a screwdriver.

"You all think this is funny, but Kage's life could be in danger. Think about that as you're getting your jollies off keeping me locked up. If anything happens to him, I'm holding the agency responsible. I'll...I'll perform a citizen's arrest and have every one of you thrown in jail. Even you, Garrett. I don't care if you're my brother!" she shouted.

Out of breath, her toe killing her, she sat down on the bed. The silence was unbearable. She had no idea what was going on outside the room or how things were going at the meeting. Heaviness settled in her chest, and her vision blurred. She rubbed her eyes. She was not going to cry.

She had to think. There had to be some way for her to get out of the room.

Much later, she still hadn't come up with a plan. She'd given the boys the silent treatment so they'd quit trying to initiate any kind of conversation with her. She lay back on the bed, hugging the pillow to her chest. Damn them.

The door clicked. Jane rolled over to see Charlene and Sabrina hurry into the room. She jumped up and lunged for the door, but Tony slammed it shut before she could manage an escape. She smacked her palm against the metal.

"Come here, honey." Charlene grabbed Jane's shoulders and gathered her in a hug. "Everything is going to be okay."

"No, it's not." She laid her head on Charlene's shoulder, exhausted. "I'm worried. Kage is all by himself."

Sabrina threw her arms around them both and joined the group hug. "We've known Kage a long time. He's more than capable of handling things."

Jane lifted her head. "You don't understand. He swore he'd never turn out like his family. He doesn't even break the speed limit. People think the worst about him, and he walks away. He never confronts them or fights to prove he's a good and decent person. I don't want him doing something he'll regret for the rest of his life because of me."

Sabrina rubbed Jane's back. "Try to think positively."

"I know he'll put himself in harm's way to make this right." Jane pulled away. "He said he'd do anything to keep me safe. *Anything.*"

"Lord save us," Charlene whispered. "We need to figure out how to get out of here before that boy does something he'll regret." She paused. "Well, you can't go alone. There's safety in numbers."

"So, you'll help me?" Hope filled her, and she held out her arm.

Charlene clasped her hand. Then Sabrina laid her hand on top of theirs. Jane gave them a shaky smile. Together they might be able to overtake the guys and find Kage.

"This place is built better than a jail cell, and the boys are under strict orders from Kage not to let me out." She leaned forward and lowered her voice. "We'll have to figure out what will make them go against Kage's wishes. It'll have to be something big."

"I could be claustrophobic." Charlene peered around the room and fanned her face. "I might be, because it's hotter than hell in here, isn't it?"

Jane patted Charlene's hand. "No, you're probably having a hot flash."

"Shut your mouth." Charlene scoffed. "Only time a woman should get one of those is in bed with a hot-looking man, and it's been a month since that's happened to me."

"Who?" Sabrina leaned back, eyeing Charlene. "I didn't even know you dated."

Charlene lowered her gaze and bristled. "Don't have to date to have a good time, sugar."

Jane glanced from Sabrina to Charlene. She shook her head, getting the image Charlene planted in her head out of the way to concentrate on more important things. "Come on, you two. We need a plan that won't fail, because we only have one chance to trick them."

"Well, Garrett ignores me half the time, so I'm no help." Sabrina held her hand out, palm facing the door, and admired her nails. "I doubt if he'd even notice if I stripped down to the slinky black thong I bought yesterday."

"Oh please, he's a man. Of course he would." Jane rolled her eyes. "We need something bigger and more dramatic…an emergency of some kind."

"Do you still use one of those breather things?" Charlene looked at Sabrina and held her hand to her mouth, pinching her finger and thumb together.

Sabrina wrinkled her nose. "An inhaler? No, I grew out of my asthma phase ten years ago. The doctor said it wasn't uncommon once you went through puberty. They believed the condition was hormonal or something like that."

Jane whispered, "Does Garrett or the boys know you don't use one anymore?"

Sabrina shrugged. "Did they even know I had one in the first place? I was pretty young. I don't think they paid any attention to me when I was at your house."

"Even better, because it'll take them by surprise." She stood. "You're going to fake an asthma attack. Charlene and I will go hysterical, thinking you're going to die. I'll yell for Garrett. There's no way he won't come in if he thinks something is medically wrong with you. When he opens the door, act like you can't breathe."

"What do I do?" Charlene asked.

Jane smiled. "Hold on to me and don't let me chicken out. We'll act scared, and Garrett will rush to Sabrina, who'll be lying on the floor. When he's distracted, we'll make a run for it."

She grabbed Sabrina and led her over to the corner. "Lie down and pull up your skirt.

"Exactly what will that do?" Sabrina looked back at her.

"If Garrett doesn't fall for the medical emergency, maybe he'll fall for a slinky black thong." She grinned. "Now hurry. I want to get out of here and find Kage. Once Garrett realizes what we've done, slip away, and drive your car around the block. I doubt if we can get far. You'll need to pick us up. Once we're together again, we'll hunt down Kage."

A shiver crawled up her spine. If anything went wrong or Scott spotted her, she was putting them all at risk. But she had to hope that he wouldn't act if she was with other people.

She moved over to Charlene and squeezed her hand. With no more delay, she took a deep breath and screamed. She motioned for Sabrina to start her act. "Sabrina, oh my God. Sabrina!"

Loud wheezes and a fit of coughing came from her friend. Jane studied Sabrina's face as it reddened at a rapid pace. For a second she wondered if anyone had pretended an asthma attack and forced a real one to come on. Sabrina was *that* good.

"Help," she yelled, moving to the door. "Garrett, open the damn door. Sabrina can't breathe. She needs her inhaler." She pounded on the steel. "Charlene, help her. Garrett, get in here!"

The doorknob turned. Garrett filled the frame and took in Sabrina writhing on the floor, the hem of her skirt around her waist showing off a sexy pair of panties and a sound like a sea lion during mating season emanating from her lips. Garrett's hard face softened and he cussed under his breath, moving forward without giving Jane or Charlene a glance.

"You have to help her. She has asthma, and was complaining about how she couldn't catch her breath." Jane pushed Garrett faster, but he was already focused entirely on Sabrina.

The moment Garrett went down on one knee to come to Sabrina's rescue, Jane grabbed Charlene's hand and tugged her out the door.

"Come on, we'll sneak out through the garage," she whispered.

Hope fueled her forward. She had no idea how to find Kage, but Bay City wasn't that large of a town, so she had to try.

Chapter Sixteen

Across town, in an abandoned airplane hangar, Kage stood in front of underground drug lord Darrell Archer. Three armed men stood several feet away, eyes averted, yet keyed in to his every move. Ten minutes after walking through the unlocked door, Darrell had yet to bring up Kage's reasons for requesting the meeting.

Dressed in a gray suit, burgundy shirt, and black tie, Darrell rocked back on his heels and folded his arms, one hand going to his chin. Kage stood perfectly still, feet wide, shoulders relaxed, hands at his sides. His easy posture belied the tightness in his gut and the bitter taste of disgust on his tongue.

The years hadn't changed his uncle. All the Archer men carried the strong square jaw line, steel eyes, and the ability to hide what they were thinking. Darrell exhibited a quiet power that most men wouldn't trust. The resemblance between Darrell and Kage's father unnerved Kage, and he knew others perceived him the same way because he carried the familiar facial features that marked them as family. He'd felt it his whole life.

"You're a disappointment, Kage." Darrell sighed heavily. "It's been what…twelve, thirteen years since you've seen your dad?"

"Fifteen," he said. "Since the day the cops pulled him out of the house."

Darrell clicked his tongue. "What a shame. Your dad worked hard in the business to provide you a home, a future, security. He proved his loyalty when trouble came and he took the fall, so the underground could rebuild and prosper. He wasn't only protecting what is rightfully ours, he's doing time for *you*. He expected you to step into his role beside me. And this is how you choose to pay him back? By not even visiting him in the penitentiary? Refusing to acknowledge your family?"

Kage forced himself not to show any emotion. "While you might want to rehash the good intentions of our family to keep the West Coast in heroin, women, and crime, I've come here for a different purpose."

Darrell studied him, and as if he found Kage's declaration funny, he laughed. "You've been gone a long time. Have you forgotten so completely how things are done?"

Every time Kage closed his eyes, every detail of his life played over in his mind. No matter how much he wanted to forget where he came from, he couldn't hide from the truth.

He disregarded the question. "I need to know where and how to contact a man."

"Your ties to the police bureau can't help you out?" Darrell asked. "That's what you went to college for? Son, the education you could've received free, from me, would've allowed you to keep your self-respect, and you wouldn't have had to crawl back to me now."

"I know who I'm dealing with." Kage stepped forward. "He runs with someone tied to the underground, and that's information you can get me. Information you *owe* me."

Darrell's eyes turned hard. "Careful, Kage. I don't let anyone threaten me, including my own blood."

"You owe me," he repeated, his voice deathly quiet. "I'm calling a marker on my mom's death."

Darrell narrowed his eyes, and Kage felt the anger rolling off his uncle. He'd saved his one get-out-of-jail-free card for almost twenty years.

The evidence concerning his mother's death would mean nothing now, all these years later, but blood was blood. Calling his mark was the one thing he had on his uncle. At nine years old, he'd witnessed his mom's death. He'd watched his uncle hand the heroin to his mom and stand over her as she shot the drug in her vein, instantly stopping her heart.

He'd kept Darrell's secret from the police, from his dad, from everyone. All because he knew that, someday, he'd need it to keep himself out of the dirty business of his family. He'd selfishly protected himself instead of bringing his vendetta down in his mom's name.

Darrell's mouth tightened and he walked away. He stopped and pivoted back around without coming any closer. "Name?"

"Scott Carson," he said.

At the mention of Scott, the already tense atmosphere seemed to spike a notch higher. Darrell's eyes moved from one of his men to the ground and back to Kage. "You're calling in the marker?"

He dipped his chin. "Yes."

"And it's only information you seek? You're not asking for him to disappear?" Darrell asked.

Kage would like nothing more than to know Scott was dead to the world. "He hurt my woman. I want to take him down myself."

Darrell smirked. "Finally, I see my blood runs in your veins when it comes to women. An Archer through and through."

Kage refused to acknowledge he was out for murder, nor would he deny he and Darrell were related. His boot heavy with the pistol, he shifted his stance. Darrell's men were aware he was carrying weapons. For reasons unknown to him, they had allowed him to keep them. His fingers itched. He'd love to put a bullet in Darrell's forehead as well and pay him back for what he'd done to his mom.

An addict and dependent on anyone she could attach herself to, his mom would've probably ended up dead in a few more years, but she was his mother. At one time, she was his world, and along with all the bad, there were good times he remembered.

"I see." Darrell inhaled deeply. "Well, then I can give you the information you're seeking."

"The name of his boss…" Kage's skin tingled.

Darrell lifted his chin and studied Kage for several seconds. "He works for me."

Uncontrolled anger seized him. The muscles in his face constricted and he turned, unable to look at this man. The man who'd played judge and jury to innocent people. Kage screamed inside for the pain he'd lived through, the horror of what he'd seen, the guilt laying on his shoulders from those affected. Nobody came away happy, healthy, whole.

He thought of Jane and how he'd pushed her away, only to have his past collide with hers anyway. He'd thought her safe in Pullman, but even there, his uncle was fucking with those he cared about, trying to rip everyone away from him. His mother put herself firmly in the hands of his uncle, relying on him for her next fix. His father, a man he had admired as a kid, had foolishly stood by his brother, disregarding the safety of his wife, his son, and his freedom.

Who was next: Garrett? Tony? Lance? Charlene? There was no stopping his uncle's destruction. Darrell wouldn't be satisfied until he had Kage under his control.

"I made you a promise all those years ago," Darrell said. "There's no escaping your heritage. You're a part of me no matter how much you try and deny it."

Kage whipped his gaze to his uncle. "I am *nothing* like you."

Darrell's swift inhale was the only sign that he heard, yet he continued. "No. You're stronger, smarter, and loyal."

Kage curled his fingers. There was no way this would end well. No matter what he decided, Jane would lose him. He had to make a choice. Walk away, always waiting for the next devastating blow, or take out the man responsible for the pain.

"I can see what you're thinking, Kage. Make it simple. You know what you have to do." Darrell stepped forward. "Your mother was too weak to survive. I told my brother, he should never have married her. That she was—"

Kage squatted, going for his pistol as three simultaneous *clicks* echoed in the hangar. His eyes flicked to Darrell's men. They were all armed and pointing their weapons at him as he remained crouched, holding the gun on Darrell.

No matter what kind of woman his mom was, she was still his mother. "Don't ever speak about my mother again or I'll kill you."

"You've used your last marker, son. You have none left. My men will shoot on my command." Darrell stepped forward. "The next time I see you, we'll be on even ground. It's not too late to come on board. We're family. I can protect you."

Kage straightened, lowering his arm but keeping his finger on the trigger. "Never."

Then he turned around and walked out of the building. He had what he came for. Now he could move forward. Scott was a dead man walking.

The whole ride back to the garage, he pushed his family problems out of his mind. The significance of handing over the one thing that'd kept Darrell away from him paled in comparison to keeping Jane safe.

Today's meeting proved he'd never be rid of the threat. He punched the steering wheel. He'd never join Darrell in business. Period.

If anyone else would've been running Scott, he could've planned, invaded, and taken them both out. But since it was his uncle, he'd have no help taking Carson down. The depth of power Darrell had behind him was too great. He'd have to trust his leverage—that his uncle would bring Scott to him without his having to join the family. He'd never take Jane or his friends down that road.

He pulled into the lot and summed up the scene in one glance. The Harley and the Camaro were parked in the same spots. He threw open the door. Sabrina and Charlene's vehicles parked as well.

Jane alone was trouble. Those three women together meant total chaos.

Chapter Seventeen

The running air compressor in bay 2 muffled whatever Tony was yelling at the women. Jane held the hose with the grinder attached in front of her, her finger on the throttle, creating more noise and a wicked weapon if anyone came close.

"Get back!" She motioned her head for Sabrina to throw the next weapon.

A former pitcher for her college softball team, Sabrina held the wrench in front of her, wound up, and let it fly underhanded toward Tony. Jane rolled her eyes as Tony easily swept to the side and missed being hit. All the boys had been athletes in their own right. The girls would have to try something else.

"Charlene, hand me the paint gun…no, not that one, the one on the ground." Jane became more determined at the possibilities the paint gun presented. They'd interrupted Lance painting, and he hadn't had time to drain and clean the gun. With any luck, there was enough midnight blue spray to get them out of there.

She'd thought Sabrina's fake asthma attack would have been enough to get them past the men. While Garrett hung back to see if Sabrina needed help, she and Charlene snuck out of the room. But her decision to lead them out through the garage, thinking the others were in the office, backfired when they ran into Lance and Tony working on cars.

Charlene brought her the paint canister, and Jane quickly unscrewed the grinder. A benefit of growing up with a dad who was a mechanic, she knew her way around tools.

At that moment, the charge for the compressor shut off and the garage went silent. She smiled in victory. A full tank of air, an almost full canister of paint, and she was taking them down.

"Dammit, Jane. Don't do it." Garrett moved toward her. "That's a special-ordered paint. The customer wants his car delivered next week."

"Back off." She held the paint gun in front of her. "You have two choices. One, we cause more damage than you can comprehend, or two, you step back and open up the garage door and let us out. What's it going to be?"

"Three. You put down the fucking paint gun. That's a ten-thousand-dollar paint job on a seventy-thousand-dollar car behind you." Garrett glared. "You get one drop on that vehicle, and you'll be working the rest of your life to pay me back."

Oops. She glanced behind her. "It's not one of your classics?"

He shook his head. She flipped her ponytail behind her shoulder. Just great. Her one move defeated, she went for the next big thing.

"Garrett…I have to help Kage. You know what will happen if he goes through with whatever he's got planned. I won't let him get hurt." She set down the paint gun and approached her brother. "Come with me. We can't let him make a mistake he'll regret."

Tony cleared his throat. She turned to see Kage standing behind him in the doorway. Relief swept through her, leaving her weak, and she reached out to hold on to Garrett.

Kage stalked toward her, she toward him, breaking into a run once it hit her that he was okay. He was safe. She buried her head in his chest, holding him tight. Going by the wildness in his gaze, whatever he'd gone through, he needed her.

When a final shudder rocked his body, she leaned back, checking him over from head to toe before settling on his face. His eyes softened and she breathed through the tightness in her chest.

Standing in front of him, she gazed up into his face. "You're back."

"You're not in the holding room," he said.

"Kage, I couldn't—"

His mouth came down on hers, hard, hot, and moist. She clutched his shirt, holding on. Nothing else existed.

He pulled back as suddenly as he had started. "I like how much you worried about me, baby."

She melted even more, her arms tightening around his waist. He was okay.

His hand slid along her back to her nape. He squeezed lightly. "I'm so damn glad to have you in my arms."

She poked him in the chest while keeping a firm hold on him with her other arm. "Don't ever do that to me again!"

He grinned. She tried to glare, but the relief of having him back made it impossible to appear stern. Her earlier anger over the trick he'd played no longer mattered. He was safe and okay.

His cheek twitched. "Baby…"

"There's nothing funny about this situation." She stepped away, looking around. "We were all worried. I pimped Sabrina off on Garrett and made her show her sexy thong and forced Charlene to run in her heels. I almost ruined a customer's car. I was willing to do anything to get to you." She fisted her hands on her hips.

He continued to smile at her. She found her resolve weakening when he looked at her as if she could do nothing wrong. She moved forward, and he hooked his finger in the belt loop of her jeans and pulled her closer.

"Are you two done?" Garrett shook his head, but even he grinned, and she understood his happiness. He loved Kage like a brother. "Let's brief."

"Cool." Sabrina walked to Garrett and looped her hand through his arm. "You heard the man. Let's brief."

"Oh, hell no," Garrett muttered, causing all the boys to grin.

Kage pulled on Jane's jeans and kept her beside him as they walked out of the garage and into headquarters. She followed him to his desk and sat on his lap. Not that she had a choice. He pulled her down and wrapped his arms around her waist.

She snuggled closer, and he sighed deeply. "Thanks for giving me this, Janie. I need you right now."

"You've got me, honey," she whispered.

That's when she noticed the stiffness in his body and the slight quiver in his arms. She leaned back, wanting to help him. Her stomach clenched as she realized she had no idea what he'd gone through.

"I'll remind you all that we have nonagency members in the room." Garrett sat behind a computer, ignoring Sabrina, who perched on the edge of his desk. "Agency business is private. Let's keep it that way."

"Don't hold back, sugar." Charlene removed her half sweater, displaying an impressive amount of cleavage before planting her butt in a chair. "If this involves Jane, we want to hear everything. No more secrets."

Tony leaned back in the chair, clasped his hands behind his head, and swung his feet up on his desk. "Next thing they'll want to do is go out on stakeouts. I want it on the record that I'll quit if any one of you even shows up when I'm working."

"Can we do that?" Sabrina leaned over the desk toward Garrett.

"No." Garrett's gaze swept her body from head to toe. "What are you doing here?"

"Wherever Jane goes, I go. We're back together, if you haven't noticed." Sabrina crossed her legs, swung her foot, and it was obvious to Jane that she was staying put. "Nothing will break our friendship apart again."

"Hell." Garrett looked to Kage. "Go on. Jane will tell her anyway, and we might as well have everyone prepared and on guard."

"Yes." Sabrina pumped her fist in the air.

"What you hear stays in this room." Garrett pinned her with a look. "If I have to, I'll make you sign a waiver and I *will* come after you if I hear of anything that's been leaked outside the agency."

"Really?" Sabrina leaned toward Garrett. "Tell me, what kinds of things will you do if you catch me?"

"Sabrina." Garrett growled. "This is serious."

Sabrina nodded, the humor evaporated. "I know. I want to help."

"Okay." He waited, and when Sabrina remained silent, he continued, "Kage, update us on what's going on."

Kage locked his fingers together, tightening his hold on Jane. "Carson works for my uncle."

Jane wasn't sure if it was her own heartbeat echoing in the room or Kage's she heard. She strained to face him, but he held her in place. *Scott works for Kage's uncle?*

"I'll give him two days to show himself and if he doesn't, I'll go underground," Kage said. "My uncle won't deny me entrance, because he'll be too glad to have me back under his control. I'm worth more than one of his men. Despite his fucked-up ways, family still comes first to him."

"You can't." Garrett shrugged, looking around the room at the other boys. "Not alone. We're in this together."

"Impossible. Even the feds are unable to get into the inner circle.

It has to be me." Kage stood, never releasing his hold on Jane. "I'll be in and out. Over."

"They'll never let you out alive," Garrett said.

"Wait." Jane squeezed Kage's arms. "You're talking about turning and going into your family's business. You can't do that."

"Not your decision," Kage murmured.

"Are you kidding me? It's totally my call. This is about me. I won't let you." She pushed at his hands. "Let me go."

She whirled and faced the others. "Do *not* let him do this."

"Sis…" Garrett rubbed the back of his neck. "What he's saying makes sense. He's the only one who has the connections to get to Scott."

"Have you lost your mind?" She marched over and stood beside Charlene. "All of us know he doesn't want anything to do with his family."

No one answered her. She turned to Charlene. "Tell them."

"Honey…" Charlene lowered her chin and her voice. "You have to let him do what he has to do."

Jane's jaw dropped opened. This could not be happening.

Kage had fought his whole life to prove he was nothing like his father, his uncle, his mother. She'd heard the talk around town. If he went underground, for her, he'd lose everything he'd struggled to build for himself. He was the most law-abiding person she knew.

"We're done here." Kage scooted his chair under the desk. "I'm taking Janie home."

When he reached her side and held out his hand, she folded her arms. He couldn't declare the subject finished, because she wasn't through yet. No way was she going to allow him to take a bullet for something she had caused.

"Hang on." Sabrina jumped off the desk. "It's still early and I'm starving after all that excitement. Let's go out for breakfast. We haven't hung out together since Jane and I left for college."

Garrett shook his head. Lance and Tony stood. Kage looked at Jane and asked, "Hungry?"

She wasn't ready to be alone with Kage until she had a plan. "Yeah."

"We're in." Kage threw his arm across her shoulders. "Garrett?"

"You owe me." Garrett grabbed the keys off the counter, a scowl on his face.

Her brother's attitude seemed out of place. She leaned into Kage. "What's his problem?"

He chuckled. "I'll explain later."

Mashed between the others, she walked squeezed side by side with Kage until they reached his car. She slid into the front seat. They'd all agreed to meet at the bar where Charlene said she'd whip them up some breakfast. Kage let the other cars go first before following in the Mustang.

Jane squeezed his hand, loving that part of him that pushed away his family problems and relied on the Beaumont Body Shop guys to help him remain on this side of the law—his ability to do the right thing no matter how dangerous his job became. It gave her hope that good guys always came in first and bad guys would lose. Soon their problems would be over, and she wanted to spend a lifetime giving him the same comfort he freely gave her every single day.

Chapter Eighteen

A few stragglers wandered into Corner Pocket to pick up the free cup of coffee Charlene always handed out during morning hours and then quickly left, leaving the seven of them mostly alone in the bar. Jane leaned back in the booth, her shoulder against Kage's arm. Garrett sat on her other side, closest to the window. Both men were suffocating her with their overprotectiveness.

"Charlene, sit down and eat." She pointed to the chair at the end of the booth. "You overdid it on the hash browns. I'm stuffed."

"Coffee's good for me. I'm not young anymore, and anything I eat goes straight to my hips." Charlene sat down and looked at Kage. "Guess this is as good a time as any to ask you what you're doing."

Kage placed his hand on Jane's thigh. "I wait, and if that doesn't work, I go underground."

Charlene waved off his answer. "Not about that. You and Jane. Any other time, I'd let you two figure this out for yourself, but considering what she's been through, her daddy out of the picture, and"—she pointed at Garrett—"him too wrapped up in his own life. Someone needs to watch out for her."

"Charlene..." She rolled her eyes.

"Don't 'Charlene' me." She sipped her coffee. "I'm serious. You're coming off a long-term relationship with a man who is up to no good and treated you worse than dog shit. It's been a week since you moved into Kage's house, and look at you two. You can't keep your hands off each other."

"Well…it just took me a while to realize how much I missed being away. Now that I have him back in my life, I do want to be with him," Jane said.

"Jane's right. She's back, and I'm not going to waste any more time away from her." Kage leaned closer to Charlene. "But I will give you my word, I'll never hurt her."

"I didn't think you would. I know you better than that, Kage." Charlene peered over the edge of her mug. "I'm talking about her heart. Don't you break it, or I'll come after you."

"Geez." Jane shook her head. "My life has turned into a TV drama."

"You have my word," Kage said quietly.

"I'll vouch for him, Charlene." Garrett threw his arm around Jane. "We've talked. Kage is cool with everything and knows he'll answer to me if he hurts my sister. Leave them alone now."

Jane had to remind herself that she was a grown woman, past the age of being upset if someone didn't agree with her choices, and recognizing their nosiness as concern over her happiness. She'd get over her embarrassment, because her behavior recently gave them a right to doubt her ability to take care of herself. She'd proven how incompetent she was in that respect when she fell for Scott's lies and continued to take his abuse. Not to mention how hard it was for her to accept help from her friends and family. Her eyes burned with unshed tears. She only wished she could move on from her mistakes.

She had to wonder if Kage fully trusted her.

For four years, she'd told everyone lies. She'd made excuses for what her life had become. She closed her eyes briefly. "Do I even want to know what went down between you two?"

Kage and Garrett answered together. "No."

"This is awesome." Sabrina elbowed Tony. "Isn't this great?"

Tony winked. "I'm feeling all soft and gushy."

"Me too." Sabrina sighed, missing Tony's sarcasm. "What you need to do is go out on a date. Just the two of you, so you can have a night off from all the madness in your lives."

"Kill. Me. Now." Jane groaned, staring a hole in Sabrina.

"Good idea," Kage said.

Jane sat straighter. "What?"

He had to be kidding. With everything going on with Scott, Kage meeting his uncle this morning, and her unable to take two steps away from any one of them, he wanted to go out on a date?

Kage turned his big body in the booth to face her. "I'm taking you out tonight."

"You're serious?" she whispered.

"As a heart attack, baby." He lowered his voice. "I want to pull Carson out into the open, piss him off. If he sees me out with you, he'll take it personally and lose his cool."

"Can we talk about this in private?" she asked.

Kage's gaze left her and sought out Garrett. She studied her brother. "Don't tell me you want us to go out too," she said.

Garrett leaned closer. "If Kage draws him out, we'll be around. He'll have backup. It'll be safer than letting him go alone."

Every scenario of what could happen if they went out as a couple played in her head. None of them were good, and all of them scary. Doing that not only risked Kage's life but Garrett's, Lance's, and Tony's too.

"No." She pushed against Kage. "Move. I want out."

"You can't walk away." He hooked his hand behind her neck.

"Get it through your head. Until this is over, someone is always with you. The sooner we can get this asshole, the safer you are. You can have back your life of coming and going when you want."

"At whose expense?" She slapped the table. "You're asking me to risk one of you getting hurt or worse. I keep telling you...you have no idea what he's capable of doing. I should've stayed in Pullman. If I knew you"—she pointed around the table—"any of you, were going to act this way, I never would've come home."

Kage's mouth hardened. He stared at her until she wanted to scream and then slid out of the booth across the bar. She gasped as he smacked the swinging door and disappeared out of sight. Her body froze, and all she could do was stare at the exit. She'd never seen such fury on his face.

"Sis, you need to—"

"I've got to go." She slid out of the booth.

Lance rose and blocked her from going after Kage. "Can't do that, Jane."

"Shut up and move." She pushed against his chest, but he didn't budge. "Let me out."

Garrett grabbed her arm and she swung out at him. "Did you see the look on his face?"

"Yeah." He pulled her a few tables away and put her in another booth before sitting down, effectively blocking any escape. "We need to talk. Privately."

She wrapped her arms around her waist and leaned against the table. Her legs trembled, and she bit down on her lip. "Let me talk to him first."

"Right now you need to give him time to check himself. A few minutes, that's all he'll need," Garrett said.

"Why?"

He held her hand. "He's afraid of scaring you. Up until now, he had hold of his temper. Finding out what happened to you riled him. I've never seen him lose his cool before, but he saw blood when he found out Scott put his hands on you. He doesn't want you to deal with his anger and get the wrong impression. Sis, he's having a hard time. We all are. It's not right that Carson got away with abusing you this long. Kage doesn't want to add to what you've gone through."

"But he'd never hurt me," she said.

He smiled tenderly. "I know that, but Kage's protecting you. He doesn't believe that others see him the same way that we do. So, he walks away and checks himself."

"I need to go to him," she whispered. "I'll talk to him. I can calm him down."

"Sis, there's things about Kage you need to know." Garrett sighed. "This morning he met with his uncle."

"I figured that out already, between the talking in code and the mysterious looks, but I want to talk to Kage," she said.

"Dammit, will you sit still and listen." Garrett ran his hand through his hair. "What you don't know is, it's a do-or-die situation with his family. They believe since he's blood, he's one of them. Kage stepping into their circle means he can't walk away."

"But he won't let it get that far. He's not a criminal. He's clean."

"Darrell Archer took a marker for the information he gave Kage on Carson." Garrett stared at the table, not meeting her eyes.

"Marker?" she whispered.

"A favor. Kage had something, whether that was information or whatever, he didn't say, that had kept his uncle away from him all these years. Now he has nothing to keep Darrell from coming after him, and he *will* come. The life Kage has lived is tainted, because he will never know when his uncle will use him or get rid of him if he thinks Kage's trying to take him down. Men like that...they have ways of making people disappear. That marker kept Kage safe, and now he doesn't have that insurance to protect himself." Garrett leaned back and gazed at her. "Do you understand what I'm telling you?"

Her stomach seized and she covered her mouth, gagging. Garrett cussed and pulled her out of the booth, across the bar, and pushed her into the bathroom. She barely made it to the toilet before she lost her breakfast.

Tears rolled down her face, but she blamed it on getting sick. Inside, she was dying. Nothing. Not one single thing Scott did to her was as awful as hearing what Kage gave up to keep her safe. She didn't deserve it.

Charlene and Sabrina rushed into the bathroom. She let them help her clean her face, murmuring soothing words as they surrounded her. But all she could think about was Kage and how she'd ruined his life.

"Are you okay?" Sabrina rubbed Jane's arms. "We'll help you get through this, and that jerk will regret ever hurting you."

She let Sabrina pull her into a hug and hold her. "This is all my fault."

"Bullshit." Charlene turned off the faucet and brought her a paper towel. "Dry your face. That ex-boyfriend of yours will pay. I don't want to hear another word from you taking the blame for what he's done."

The door opened and Kage stood just inside the entrance. She flinched, pulling away from Sabrina. His gaze swept over her body, landing on her face. His anger from earlier was nothing compared to right now.

His eyes softened, belying the tension around his mouth. His jaw muscle ticked and his chest expanded. "You okay?"

She shook her head.

"Come on. I'll take you home." He spoke softly, holding out his hand.

She walked with him out into the bar, past the others, and straight outside. She allowed him to buckle her seat belt before walking to the opposite side and taking the wheel. As they drove off, he held her hand. She squeezed his fingers, afraid more than ever she was going to lose him.

When they arrived at Kage's, she stopped him from opening his car door. "Is it true? Will your uncle come after you?"

"He'll try." He relaxed back in the seat.

"Kage, I can't let you live the rest of your life worried…like I am. Give him back the marker or whatever it's called," she said.

"Can't." He brought her hand up to his lips and kissed her knuckles. "It's over."

"But you need to keep yourself safe."

"I'll only say this once, baby." He locked his gaze on her. "There's one thing more important than watching my own back or worrying about what'll come my way because I had the misfortune of being an Archer."

"What?" she whispered.

"You."

She melted. Then the guilt hit her whole body, overwhelming her. "Oh, Kage, I can't—"

He grabbed her head, pulled her forward, and kissed her hard. The multitude of emotions left her feeling as if she were swimming in the ocean, the tide pulling her away from shore, and all the breath she'd had left to scream for help had fled.

"Let's go rest up for tonight, and then I want you to get dressed in your best clothes," he said.

"W-what?" she breathed, because surely she was drowning.

"We've got a date. It's a little late considering, but it's our first one, and I want to take my woman out on the town." He opened the car door.

As he walked around the front of the Mustang, she shivered. And not out of fear for how fast they were taking things.

She was going out on a date with Kage.

Chapter Nineteen

Kage's bedroom resembled a dressing room at Saks, minus the mirrors and complimentary coffee. Jane stood next to the bed in the ninth of the dresses Sabrina had brought to the house for her to try on in an attempt to fancy her up for her first date with Kage. The red stretchy material hugged her curves, its short skirt ending at the middle of her thighs.

The thin straps allowed a deep V in the front and its scooped back dipped to an almost indecent level just above her ass. She twisted her upper body, studying her exposed flesh.

"My back dimples are showing. Kage isn't even going to see the dress, he'll be staring at my back all night," she said.

"Girl, that's hot. I'd give anything to have your dimples. Kage is going to go ballistic." Sabrina sat down on the floor and opened a shopping bag. "I've got the perfect shoes too."

"I have bigger feet than you. I'll never be able to wear them." She eyed her favorite boots, the ones she had worn when she ran away from Scott. "I need something I can wear those with, or my sneakers. The clothes I left at the house when I went away for college don't include high heels."

"You're only a half a size bigger than me. You can handle a little discomfort for a couple of hours." Sabrina held up a pair of red four-inch heels with a black spike. "Here they are. I bought them to go with the dress for Tiffany's wedding last year."

"Tiffany Winters?" Jane sat down on the edge of the bed, remembering the lead cheerleader who led the fashion pack at Bay City High. "Who'd she marry?"

"Tyler Schooner," Sabrina said.

"Get out!" Jane laughed, holding up her foot for Sabrina to put on the shoe. "He always had his head buried in a chemistry kit."

"Not anymore. He's gorgeous and the proud daddy of a little girl." Sabrina stepped back. "Perfect. Try to walk in them."

Jane stood and tottered. In a borrowed dress and shoes, excitement filled her. Scott had forbidden her to wear anything with an ounce of sexy in it the last two years. His idea that she was not to attract another man's attention went to the level of paranoid.

"How do they feel?" Sabrina asked.

Jane walked to the dresser and back, finding her balance. "Okay. They're a little tight in the toes, but the heel doesn't rub."

"I told you they'd work for you." Sabrina moved to pick up the mess they'd made in their mad search to find Jane something to wear.

A knock came at the door. Sabrina scrambled to it and peeked out. "You can't come in."

"Why not?" Kage said.

"Because she has to make an entrance. It's a girl thing. You have to pretend you're not picking her up in your bedroom." Sabrina glanced over her shoulder and rolled her eyes at Jane. "He's sexy, but he's clueless on how women work."

"Reservations are in a half hour," Kage said.

"She'll be ready. Just go...my God, you look hot." Sabrina whistled. "Does Garrett ever clean up and wear anything like that?"

"Um, you'd have to ask him," Kage said. "Is she going to be ready in time?"

"Of course. Go out in the living room. She'll come to you." Sabrina slammed the door and faced Jane. "Makeup. Now!"

As promised, Kage steered clear of the bedroom to give her time to prepare. In ten minutes, Jane put on her makeup, spritzed perfume on her lower back so as not to stain the dress, and left the room. Sabrina said her goodbyes.

Jane hesitated in the hallway and pressed her hand to her stomach. She hadn't expected butterflies, but there they were, fluttering on sunshine.

A deep breath and a prayer she didn't make a fool of herself, she stepped out into the living room. All worries left her. Kage stood beside the couch watching her.

In a navy suit, cream-colored shirt and red tie, he'd transformed into a man who ate CEOs for breakfast. His stubborn lock of hair already rebelled and flopped down on his forehead. His gaze warmed, and she knew he liked what he was seeing. She ducked her chin, her heart racing. Oh, wow.

"Baby?"

She caught her lip between her teeth and raised her eyes to him. He came to her and, instead of taking her hand, he walked around her. Behind her, he sucked in his breath and his hand went to her back.

Braless, she swiftly inhaled at the slight touch against her skin. She froze, smiling inside, letting him take his fill of her.

"Fuck, Janie." His finger traced the slight indentions on her lower back. "You're killing me."

"Does it look all right?" she whispered, afraid he'd have her go change her outfit the way Scott always demanded when she dared buy something without his approval.

"You're beautiful. You're always beautiful, but every man tonight will see what I get to take home with me, and I'm not sure I want another man's eyes on you." He walked around her and stood in front. "Do you understand why I would want to keep you to myself?"

She swallowed. "Because you think I'll tempt a man to talk with me?"

"What?" He shook his head, putting his hands on each side of her face. "No, baby."

She frowned, and his thumbs swept her cheekbones, relaxing her facial muscles. "Did Carson make you think it was your fault if a man looked at you, talked with you?"

Because Kage forced her to look at him, she closed her eyes to hide from the truth. She knew how ridiculous Scott's demands were, and she'd fought with him over his controlling attitude more times than she could count. Sometime during their relationship—she couldn't pinpoint exactly when she'd given up—she'd stopped fighting it.

Her lack of effort to be perfect for him happened slowly, until she believed it was easier to go along with what Scott wanted. She opened her eyes and stared up into Kage's face. How could he even like the person she'd become?

"I'm sorry," she whispered.

"For what?"

"I'll go change." She moved her foot back to walk away, but he held her in place.

"You dressed for me?"

Everything about today centered on pleasing Kage, but it was also about her. She sucked in her lower lip, remembered she had lipstick on, and sighed. She wanted to dress fancy and have a good time tonight. Of course, she never forgot that their purpose of going out on date was to draw Scott out in the open.

"Yeah." Her breathing grew shallow. "I wanted to thank you for giving me the best few days of my life. I...you...I have a lot going through my head. I can't even think right, and I'm afraid I'm messing everything up."

"You're afraid." He wasn't asking, he came to his own conclusions, and he was right.

She nodded. "It's stupid, I know. I remember what I was like, but sometimes it feels like that part of me has died."

"The Janie in you," he whispered.

Again, he wasn't asking. He knew.

"Soon we're going to deal with what he's done to you, and there'll be nothing in your mind that brings him back between us. He doesn't belong inside your head, let alone touching you. When I told you that you're mine, I meant it. I also meant you'd be yourself. I know you're struggling, baby. It kills me, because you don't deserve to work through the scars Scott placed on you."

"I wasted four years, Kage. I lost my friends, my family, my dad." She shook her head. "What if it's too late?"

"It's not. I won't let it be." He wrapped her in his embrace. "You're beautiful. You'd tempt a man just by breathing, but I'm selfish. Tonight your body is for me. Those dimples are mine to enjoy. Your attention is on me, and your dress is mine."

"Well, really it's Sabrina's outfit. She's letting me borrow it," Jane whispered against his chest, her body vibrating.

His chest rumbled with laughter and he nuzzled her neck. "I'll buy her a new one, because the moment we get home, I'm going to rip it off your body and take what is mine. All of you." He trailed a finger along her cleavage. "This." His hand went around to her ass. "This."

She leaned into him. "Kage..."

"And after I'm done sampling everything..." He lowered his mouth to her ear. "I'm going to make your eyes flutter the way they do, right before you come."

"Shit," she whispered, clutching his coat in her fingers. "Do we have to go out tonight?"

He laughed again. "Yeah, baby. Let's end this shit, so we can move on to better things, huh?" He leaned back, inhaling deeply. "I have something for you before we go."

"What?" she said.

He reached into his coat pocket and pulled out a small canister the size of a one-and-a-half-inch socket. "It's Mace. Slide the lever on top to the side and squeeze the orange strip. You want to point the top at your target. Make sure you don't have it pointed up but away from you—you don't want to get that stuff in your own eyes."

She held the Mace, turning it over in her hand. "Really? It's mine?"

"Yeah." He tipped her chin, chuckling. "Will you lay off wanting a gun now and sneaking around headquarters?"

"Yes." She stood on her tiptoes in her borrowed high heels and kissed him on the lips. "Thank you. That has to be the coolest thing anyone has given me. Mace. I never would've thought to get any. I can take down Scott and watch him cry. It's perfect."

"Whoa, hang on." He shook his head, his lips twitching. "You're not to play the hero. This is in case you need it, in case someone, somehow gets near you. I don't want Carson anywhere close to you. You're mine, so I'll protect you, but if something happens, you'll have a way to defend yourself and get away. You run like hell, baby, and don't look back."

Her excitement dwindled, and she nodded. "Do you think he'll show tonight?"

"I hope." He watched her put the Mace in a small clutch purse, also borrowed from Sabrina to go with the outfit. "I want him dealt with and gone."

Chapter Twenty

On Friday nights, the Crystal Palace boasted a live quartet that'd make any man head straight to Corner Pocket for a beer. It wasn't Kage's prime choice for a date night. He'd rather hit a more intimate spot away from the high rollers who visited the casino if they were here on a real date and not drawing out Jane's ex-boyfriend.

Kage requested a table far from the music, near the windows that overlooked the Pacific Ocean. He scooted the edge of his empty plate forward and caught Lance's eye.

Lance and Garrett sat separately, one by the band, the other at the first table they'd passed as they entered the room. Their companions were oblivious to the purpose of their dates at the nicest restaurant in the casino. So far, Jane handled being the focus of everyone's attention well.

He'd worried about her blowing their plan. Her impulsive nature tended to get her in trouble, but he soon learned that if he kept his hands on her and her attention on him, she forgot she was sitting in the middle of a trap. Luckily, the atmosphere and the knowledge that they were on their first date seemed to distract her.

The waitress arrived with dessert. A chocolate something or other that looked like cake with a side of ice cream. Kage smiled at Jane's reaction.

"Next time," he murmured.

She tilted her head, her fork halfway to the cake. "What?"

"We'll do it right. Just you and me. We'll have a real date." He winked and stuck his fork in the dessert, reaching across the table to feed her a bite.

"Maybe one day we can get a room here at the hotel, and you can teach me how to play the slots down in the casino. I've never gambled before." Her smile grew and she scooted closer. "Maybe I'd win big."

"Not happening." He took his own bite of cake. "We'll go somewhere else. Not here."

"Why not?" Her back went straight, and then she dove into another bite of cake and muttered, "Sorry."

He grabbed her wrist before softening his touch and letting their hands fall to the table. "Look at me."

She wrinkled her nose. "I wasn't thinking."

"What's going through your head?" He rubbed the soft skin on the inside of her wrist. "Don't tell me what I want to hear. I want to know what you were thinking when you closed yourself off from me and apologized."

"I don't understand what you want from me," she said.

"Answer me first. Why were you sorry?"

She glanced at the tables beside them and lowered her voice. "It's expensive. We don't have to stay here."

"That's what you thought?" He grinned, finding her interpretation of his reluctance to come back to this place hilarious.

"Well, yeah. It's the swankiest place I've ever been to. I guess I got caught up in the moment and forgot we're here because"—she shrugged—"you know. We're just pretending."

His humor fled. "We sure in the hell aren't pretending. This is real, you and me. I've told you, and I'll keep telling you until you understand. I don't play games."

"Okay," she breathed. Her eyes relaxed and her breasts rose, pushing against the neckline of the dress.

He brought her hand to his lips and skimmed his mouth across her fingers. "The reason I don't want to bring you back here is because my uncle has his hands in the workings of the casino. There's a good possibility that he's downstairs right now and he's got the camera aimed at our table. I don't like him looking at what is mine."

"Oh."

He squeezed her hand. "I also don't gamble. Ever."

She nodded. "I get it."

"Do you?" He held her gaze. "All my life I've made sure I'm clean. It's not enough to be a good person. I have to rise above that and prove myself. Everyone waits, hoping, expecting me to do something to screw up so they can shake their head in pity, knowing I'm just like my father, my uncle, my mother."

"Kage—"

He stared at her. "I'd never bring you down to that level, Janie. You're too good for a place like this, despite the price tag. I will do whatever I need to do to make sure nothing about my family touches you."

"That's why you always follow the rules. Even with normal things the average person commits every day without a second thought. You don't. It's always in the back of your mind." She blinked hard, and damned if her eyes weren't filling up with tears.

"Don't, baby," he whispered. "Not with me. Never for me."

She lifted her chin and wiped all traces of pity off her face. "I get it."

"Good." He glanced across the room, caught Garrett's intense gaze, and brought his attention back to Jane. "Let's call it a night. I'm done here."

"What about Scott? He hasn't shown up yet."

Kage stood, slipped on his jacket, and walked around the table to help her out of her chair. "I'm running out of patience, and you haven't relaxed since we got here. Let's go home."

Carson might not have shown his face, but the tension in the room had never let up. Whether it was being in a place where his uncle's eyes were always watching or the anxious feeling to get this done and over with, Kage couldn't tell. He only knew Janie'd had enough, and he wanted her home where she was safe, away from his uncle, away from Scott.

Jane's step faltered near Garrett's table. Kage placed his hand on her lower back. The tension was evident in the way her spine stiffened.

"It's okay." He continued to lead her toward the front.

She leaned against his side. "Was he here the whole time?"

"Yeah." He smiled at the hostess and continued walking out the door leading to the main floor.

He walked through the large, open area of the lobby, ignoring the sounds coming from the games in the casino to their right. On high alert, his gaze swept the area as he slowed his pace. If anyone was watching, he wanted to appear as if he were full from dinner and satisfied after an evening out with his woman.

"Who else was here?" Jane looked up at him.

"Lance." He smiled and stepped toward the automatic doors. "Smile and stick with me. I'll explain when we get in the car."

He gave the valet his card. Five minutes later, they pulled away in the Mustang. He glanced at Jane. Learning they weren't alone tonight, she'd gone quiet.

"Talk," he said.

"I just want my life back and to forget I ever wasted those years with Scott." She pressed into the seat. "I'm sick of it. Sick of it all."

Kage flipped his turn signal on, drove around the corner, and accelerated onto the highway.

"Hang in there a little longer. I promise you, we'll clean this up, and Carson will no longer be a concern." He reached down and squeezed her thigh.

Jane jerked away. "He's taken everything away from me."

"Don't let him get under your skin. We have a handle on him. He can't touch you."

"He already has." Her voice rose, and she shifted in her seat. "He's still doing it, and now he's making you, Garrett, Lance, and Tony do whatever he wants. Don't you see? He won't stop, and I'll lose even more people in my life. I won't survive if someone else dies because of me."

Kage hardened, flipped on his turn signal, and slowly pulled over to the side of the highway, setting his emergency blinkers on. Then he turned toward her. "Who died?"

She clamped her lips shut and refused to look at him.

"Janie. Who died because of you?" he said.

His heart pounded. She'd given him information, and he had a firm grasp of how she'd been forced to live with Carson. But murder? That was new and important. It explained why she'd kept the truth from the agency and why she continued to protect everyone else.

The trauma from witnessing someone's death could be why she whimpered while she slept, staring at the wall long after he comforted her.

"Baby, look at me." He guided her head around and held her cheek in the palm of his hand. "Who did Carson kill?"

"I can't…not now." Her chin trembled. "I can't."

He opened his mouth, and his phone rang. "Dammit."

Shifting in his seat, he reached behind him and pulled out his phone. "Yeah?"

"There are alarms going off at your house. I've dispatched Lance and Garrett." Tony paused. "I'm locking up headquarters and heading that way. Where are you located?"

"Highway 101. We're twenty minutes away." He turned the keys and started the engine. "You'll reach there first. Hold that bastard for me."

"Got it." Tony disconnected the call.

Jane grabbed his forearm. "What's going on?"

He turned on his signal, looked behind him, and hit the highway. "Breach at the house. Alarms going off."

Her fingers tightened on him. "He's there."

"Yeah." He glanced at her. "When we get there, you stay in the car and lock the doors. Do not get out of the Mustang and do not open the door for anyone but me."

She nodded. "Okay."

He stared straight ahead. He hoped one of his men arrived first, so he didn't kill Carson with his bare hands.

Chapter Twenty-one

Kage pulled straight into the driveway of his house and parked next to his partners' vehicles. Jane lunged against the seat belt, gripping the dashboard. The front door of the house stood wide open. The lamp they left on in the living room lit up the porch.

Panic seized her. She'd forgotten her promise.

"No, no, no…" She unclipped her belt and ran out of the car before Kage pulled to a complete stop.

At the restaurant, she hadn't thought once of anything bad happening at Kage's house in their absence. She ran toward the door with only one thing on her mind. If anything happened to her cat, she'd never forgive herself.

As she reached the first step of the porch, an arm hooked her waist and her feet left the ground. She struggled.

"Dammit, calm down." Kage clamped his arms around her.

"I have to find Bluff." She kicked her legs and pushed on his arm. "She'll be scared."

"Quiet." He stalked back to the Mustang and swung her into the seat. He hovered in the door, blocking her exit. "Lock the door."

"No, please." She reached for him, but he pushed her hands back inside the car. "I need to find Bluff. I promised her. I need to find her before Scott notices I still have my cat."

"I'll get Bluff. You lock the door." He held her gaze. "Say it."

She rocked on the seat. "I'll lock the door but please, find Bluff. I can't let anything happen to her."

Kage nodded and shut Jane inside. She pushed down on the lock. "Please find her," she said, "please just find her."

Kage jogged toward the house, gun drawn, keeping his upper body low. She fisted her hands on her thighs. None of the other men showed themselves, but their vehicles parked on the front lawn and vacant meant they had to be nearby.

She wanted to go out there. Kage was more than trained to defend himself, but she needed to protect him from doing something he normally wouldn't. He was one of the good guys. He helped women, solved cases, and investigated people for a living. What he didn't do was kill people out of anger.

The personal way he took Scott's threats, because of her, she had no doubt that he'd do anything to get Scott out of her life and make him pay for what she'd gone through. She peered out the window, trying to catch a glimpse of anyone.

The late-summer sun had gone down twenty minutes ago, and without the light from the house, she could barely see a thing. The other guys should be here, but where were they?

The outside security lights came on. She inhaled a deep breath knowing Kage was responsible for lighting the area. It was one thing to face Scott alone, but the darkness made Kage vulnerable.

"Come on, Garrett. Where are you?" she whispered.

Her brother would make sure Kage stayed in control. Her hands shook. He needed backup. Scott had already proven to her the first time he came after her and hit her across the face, laying her out on the pavement, that he'd do anything if he felt justified.

Her stealing Scott's gun and money gave him a reason to kill Kage and get him out of the way. In her panic to escape, she hadn't thought about the consequences of her actions; she only wanted to get the hell away from him and find somewhere safe where he couldn't hurt her anymore.

If she left the car, maybe Scott's attention would be on her, and she could distract him, giving the boys a chance to make a move. They could catch him when his guard was down.

Kage had ordered her to stay in the car, but she'd rather face his anger than allow Scott a chance at Kage. She opened the car door. Her decision came from what she knew in her heart.

Disobeying Scott meant bruises and broken ribs. But she knew Kage would never do that. He'd be pissed for sure, but she could handle his kind of anger. She searched under the bushes in the front yard, knowing that when she was scared, Bluff tried to hide. She wanted to make sure her pet was safe before she sought out Scott.

She heard footsteps coming from inside and hurried around the corner of the house. Maybe she'd made a mistake going against Kage's wishes and getting out of the car.

Flattening herself against the side of the house, she looked expectantly toward the corner, ready to bolt if anyone came around to that side. When no one appeared, she let out the breath she'd been holding and turned to go toward the backyard. Then she gasped, and her body froze in terror.

Scott was there, pointing a gun at her, his good looks ravaged by desperation.

A few days' worth of whiskers covered his jaw, his usually groomed blond hair was messed. Even the jeans and T-shirt he wore seemed days old and slept in. She scooted back, her hand against the side of the house.

"Did you really think I wouldn't find you?" He waved the gun, never taking his aim off her.

"There are men here who'll kill you," she said.

His lip curled. "That's where you're wrong. With you here, my pistol cocked and ready, they won't dare do anything that might get you hurt."

"That's not true," she whispered.

He laughed, but no sound came out. "Where were they when you were living with me, huh? Your brother, the big investigator, too busy helping others and digging into someone else's business to give a shit about what was happening to his little sister."

She shook her head. "No."

"You have another dick between your legs." His knuckles whitened on the gun. "Do you really think Archer will save his slut of the week?"

She cringed and stepped back.

"Stop or I'll blow a hole right in your forehead," Scott said.

Where were the guys? She swallowed. With Scott's delusional state of mind, she wouldn't put it past him to shoot, unconcerned about what would happen to him when someone heard the blast.

"The first one I'll take out is the asshole who thought he could take what is mine." Scott moved closer and now she was able to see into his eyes. "Then I'm taking you back."

Jane had looked at his face for four years but had never seen the absolute rage he displayed now. Anger, yes. Disgust, yes. But for the first time, she believed he'd kill her and anyone else who stepped in his way.

"I'm sorry." She forced herself not to run away. "I'll go with you."

"You're lying, and trust me, sweetheart, you'll pay for that later." Scott stepped close enough the end of the pistol skimmed her forehead. "Get it straight in your head. I'm taking you with me whether you want to go or not. Things are changing with us. I'm not going easy on you. You've lost any trust I'd given you."

A movement behind him caught her eye. She fisted her hands at her side, afraid if she moved or looked, Scott would turn around.

"I'll show you, I can do better. I won't disobey you again," she said.

He lowered the pistol to her chest and trailed the end between her breasts. She shivered and locked her knees. Unable to get enough air in her lungs, her head swam and she feared she might actually pass out.

Kage! Garrett!

She panted, trying not to lose consciousness. Any moment, she expected to hear a gun blast, and she hoped it wasn't Scott taking her life. Or, worse, taking the life of one of the others.

"Please. I'm begging you. Take me with you," she whispered. "Please."

Kage's face came over Scott's shoulder. He stared at her but spoke to Scott. "Real easy now, drop the gun."

Kage shoved his pistol into the side of Scott's neck. Jane held her breath. Scott still had his gun against her chest.

"Please," she whispered. Whether it was begging Kage for help or asking Scott not to kill her, she had no idea.

"Put the gun down, Carson. We have you surrounded." Garrett's voice boomed behind her.

Scott laughed into her face, the sound maniacal to her ears. "Not smart, are they?"

"I'm not going to ask again. Put down the weapon slowly," Kage said.

"Do they even realize that I hold the power, sweetheart?" His hand held the pistol steady over her heart. "Let me explain what is going to happen. You all are going to step back, put down your weapons, and watch me walk away with Jane. Unless you'd like to see her life snuffed out here." He raised his brows at her. "Maybe you don't understand how you play into their lives, sweetheart. For someone who is fucking you, Archer seems to want me dead more than he wants to save your life."

Her gaze flashed to Kage. He made no move and kept his gun at Scott's neck. It wasn't true. They didn't just have sex, they'd made love. She was his woman in every sense.

"Oh, look, Archer. She's second guessing all the bullshit you've fed her." He chuckled and smiled. "My poor Jane, always doubting yourself. You don't really believe he loves you, do you?"

"Kage?" She stared at him.

She wanted to tell him she wasn't listening, and Scott was a liar. No matter what Scott said, nothing would change her mind about how she felt toward Kage, her belief in him. The hardness around Kage's mouth kept her from speaking those thoughts. Everyone knew Kage never tied himself down to one woman.

When she'd arrived back to Bay City, she'd hidden out and wallowed in self-pity. Yet he'd stepped up and taken responsibility toward her. He'd seen her at her worst. Her chest squeezed. Of course he'd protect her. She was Garrett's little sister.

"That's it, sweetheart," Scott said softly. "None of them know you the way I do. You belong with me. I'm the only one who understands the way you are. You like how I watch over you."

She gazed down at the weapon poking her in the chest, then up into Kage's face. Tears welled in her eyes. She blinked them away.

Maybe Kage wouldn't want her when he realized how much she'd changed and heard how easily it was for her to accept Scott's abuse. She wouldn't blame him. She'd done everything wrong and given Kage nothing in return. He deserved someone who came to him without any baggage. But she could prove to herself she wasn't going to add to her guilt over the past anymore.

She couldn't do this in front of the people she loved. She refused to go down letting Scott ridicule her any longer. That shit was over.

She didn't care if he shot her dead. But degrading her in front of the people she loved wasn't going to happen. Not anymore.

She cleared her throat. "Where's my cat?"

Scott's brows lowered. "Your cat?"

"Where's. My. Damn. Cat?" Her back stiffened and she raised her arm to push the gun away.

Scott grabbed her wrist, turning her, and wrapped his hand around her chest, the pistol pushed into her temple. "Walk, and if anyone thinks to shoot me, they'll be taking you out too."

Her gaze met Garrett's and he lowered his weapon, stepping back, giving Scott room. She looked at her brother, praying he understood. No one else could get hurt because of her.

His intense stare wounded her. His shoulders sagged and his mouth tightened in a grim line. She swallowed the growing lump in her throat. As she walked past him, she mouthed *I love you*.

Wanting Scott to believe she'd go without a struggle, she let him lead her to the front yard. "I need my purse."

"You don't need anything." Scott pushed her forward.

She stumbled, stepping on a rock in the grass and realized she'd lost her shoes when she jumped out of the car. They weren't even hers. She'd lost Sabrina's shoes.

"I need my purse," she said. "It's in the Mustang. I-I still have the money I stole."

The end of the gun hit her cheekbone and she cried out, trying to stay on her feet. Pain ricocheted across her nose and around her eye. She stumbled, falling against Scott. Tears blurred her vision, and the simple act of blinking nauseated her. Scott shifted directions and walked toward the car. He pivoted with his arm wrapped around her and peered inside the vehicle. "Motherfucker left his keys in the car."

"No, please," she begged.

"Stop thinking about him!" He yanked her arm. "Archer's too stupid to do anything, and now he can kiss my girl and his car good-bye. You know I love you more than he ever will. I'll teach you to forget about him. He'll never forgive you for everything you've done, but I will. We'll start over once we're away from here."

"He'll catch you, you asshole." She fought the pain and threw her weight into his side.

Her attack only pissed him off more, and he pulled her around to the driver's side. "Listen carefully. You're going to crawl through and close your door. Don't even think about running. If you do, I'll kill your brother, Archer, and those other two losers on the side of the garage. Then I'll shoot you."

She nodded, and when he leaned over, she scrambled across the driver's seat and gearshift, and into the passenger seat. Scott followed her inside.

"Shut the door." He started the engine and flipped on the lights.

She closed the door and found her purse on the floor between her feet. She picked the red bag up and set it on her lap, never taking her gaze off Scott.

"You have all the money?" Scott twisted his body. Then he put the car in reverse with his left hand without taking his aim off her.

"Yeah." She opened her purse.

Scott's laughter made her sick. She reached inside. "It's all right here."

At the end of the driveway, Scott shifted into first, put the pistol between his legs, and held out his hand. "Let's see it. I swear if there's even a hundred dollars missing, I'm going to beat the shit out of—"

She raised her hand and sprayed the Mace directly in his face. He let the clutch out and took his right foot off the gas, killing the engine as his scream filled the car.

"You bitch!" He grabbed for her but, in his blindness, he missed.

She latched onto his hair and shook his head, her vision blurred from the cloud of Mace filling the Mustang. "You can't hurt me anymore," she screamed. "I hate you."

The door flew open, and Kage was there, pulling her out to safety. Garrett, Lance, and Tony moved in, guns drawn. She rubbed the heels of her hands into her burning eyes. She was going to kill Scott.

Chapter Twenty-two

The takedown of Scott Carson lasted less than twenty seconds after his Janie used her Mace. Kage shielded Jane from the scene happening on the ground on the other side of the Mustang, making sure she was safe first. He held her arms between them to keep her from rubbing her eyes and making the sting from the Mace any worse.

She uttered not a word, but he knew it must hurt like hell.

"I'll take her in and wash out her eyes." Tony reached for Jane, giving Kage his nonverbal promise to watch over her as if she was his. "You've got five minutes. Police are on their way."

He nodded and let Tony take Jane. He waited until the front door closed and she was out of sight before heading to where Carson was being held. Fury twisted with fear over losing Janie fueled him forward with his intent to kill the man.

Garrett hovered near Carson, who sat on the ground, slumped against the wheel of the car, his hands cuffed behind his back, his eyes red and streaming, having taken a direct hit from the Mace. The cords along Garrett's neck stood out as he spoke low to Carson.

"Stand him up," Kage said.

Lance moved forward. "Check yourself, man. You do not want to go there."

He ignored the advice. "Stand him up, Beaumont, or I will."

Garrett grabbed the front of Scott's shirt, pulled him to his feet, and got in his face. "You better hope you have a long stay in prison, because I will hunt you down and make your life miserable if you even speak or think about Jane."

Scott struggled to open his eyes, squinting against the pain. "Go to hell."

Garrett turned to Kage. "You called dibs. The piece of shit is yours."

Kage stepped forward, an arm's length away from Carson. Disgust rolled through him. Most of all, he wanted to kill the man who had dared lift a hand to Jane, and probably every other woman he'd had in his life.

"Is it true? Everything you did to Jane?" he asked quietly.

Scott sneered, his eyes mere slits in a red face. "Damn right. That bitch deserved it."

Kage drew back and landed a vicious punch to Scott's ribs. The *whoosh* of breath and grunting afterward were enough evidence that he'd hit his mark. Jane wasn't going to be the only one who suffered through the agonizing pain of broken ribs. Three, if he guessed right.

"Did you force her to sleep with you?" he asked, equally quiet.

"Fuck"—Scott grunted—"off."

"Wrong answer." Kage brought his knee up and nailed Scott between the legs. Carson's eyes rolled back in his head as he slunk to the ground.

Kage pulled him up, steadying him. He leaned in and said, "You're not even worthy enough to speak her name."

He swung an uppercut to Scott's chin, sending him flying over the hood of the Mustang before hitting the ground with a sickening crunch. Carson's head rolled around as he moaned. Kage helped the asshole back to his feet and propped him against the car again. He was no way near done with the bastard yet.

"This is for all the times you made her feel less than a woman." He kicked him low in the stomach. There wasn't a spot on Carson that wasn't left hurting, but Kage still wasn't satisfied.

He wrapped his fingers over Carson's throat and squeezed. "Last, I take your life, because you touched my woman."

Satisfaction, the kind of which he'd never experienced before, gave him the strength to keep pressing in, past the muscle, past the cartilage, past the ability to breathe. Carson's body seized, stiffened, and then slumped, and still Kage continued strangling the life out of him.

"He's not worth it, man," Garrett said.

Unaware of Garrett until he spoke, Kage whipped his head to the side. "He hurt Janie," he spat out.

"Yeah." Garrett looked away. "I'm not stopping you. I'd be in your spot, killing him myself if you hadn't called rights at him first. But I also know my sister. She's been through a hell of a lot. You killing someone for her will add guilt onto what has already happened, and she will blame herself. That's the kind of woman she is. I'd prefer that you don't put that burden on her."

"Fuck," Kage breathed, letting go of the bastard.

Kage watched Carson collapse to the ground the same moment he heard the sirens coming up the lane. He turned to Garrett, wanting him to know how much he wanted to kill. How out of control he'd become. How he had the ability to become an Archer in every sense of the word. How he didn't deserve Janie.

Instead, Garrett lifted his chin. "There's a difference between you and them. There always was. Don't go there."

Kage flexed his hands and stared at Garrett. He knew. Out of all the PIs at the Body Shop, Garrett knew him the best.

For all the strength it took him to stay away from a life a crime, to turn his back on his family, and to separate himself from society. His biggest fear was that, deep down, he was capable of going over the edge. His anger, his scars, his memories burned inside of him, and he feared one day he'd have enough and go after the man who had hurt everyone he loved.

Garrett glanced down at Carson and back at Kage. "We got this covered. He went crazy. He struggled. In capturing him, he got a few injuries. You didn't see a thing. Case closed."

Turning away, Kage walked to the house and asked Tony to head outside to help Lance and Garrett. Jane sat on the couch, a wet washcloth over her eyes. He stood on the other side of the living room, soaking in the sight of her and filling his lungs with air. He'd quit breathing when he rounded the house and seen she was not in the car.

Without her, he didn't know what would happen to him. For years, she was his ideal of the perfect woman, someone to aim for and strive for so that someday he could do her proud. She was beautiful, poised, and, when some jack wasn't messing with her head, unpredictable and crazy, in the best way. The thought of having her had kept him walking the straight and narrow, and yet he almost killed a man tonight.

"Baby?" he whispered.

He wasn't sure she heard him, until she raised her head and removed the cloth from her face. Eyes swollen and vacant stared back at him. He pushed down the pain and approached her.

Already, her cheekbone showed signs of a bruise. He wanted to go back outside and put more hurt onto Carson for what he'd done. No one should ever go through what Jane did.

Sitting on the coffee table in front of her, he put her knees between his thighs and inhaled deeply. He had to tamp down the fear and vulnerability he'd experienced tonight, thinking that she could die and he'd never told her he loved her. "You okay?"

"Bluff…" She scrunched her nose. "She's gone. Tony helped me look everywhere in the house, and she's not here."

"I'll find her, baby. She could've run off into the woods. Cats are smart. She'll hide out, until she knows it's safe to come back to you." He held onto her legs, stroking the top of her thigh with his thumbs. "I know your eyes are burning something fierce, but are you hurt anywhere else?"

She laid her hand on her chest but shook her head. He removed her hand, swept her hair over her shoulder, and changed his mind about not killing Carson. A faint bruise already bloomed on her collarbone where he'd pressed the pistol to her.

"I'm fine." She glanced toward the window. "Garrett?"

"He's dealing with the police," he said.

She nodded. "Good."

"Yeah." Kage kept watching, not understanding or liking what he was seeing. "Baby?"

Jane stood. "I should put some cat food outside in case Bluff gets hungry and comes back. I wouldn't want her to go hungry."

He followed her into the kitchen. She was in shock, pretending tonight never happened. That her ex-boyfriend hadn't had a gun to her head and almost took her life.

"Do you care if I open a can of tuna too?" She poured a cup of dry cat food in a bowl.

"Go ahead," he murmured.

She gave him a smile that didn't reach her eyes. "Thanks. She'll like that. She always goes nuts when I splurge and give her moist canned cat food, and tuna is like the granddaddy of any cat dessert. She'll probably smell it from the woods, don't you think?"

Kage leaned against the archway, not answering. She had her own way of coping, and no matter what he said, she wasn't absorbing that outside her the danger was going away. Never again would she have to worry about someone coming after her or hurting her.

Jane opened the back door. Kage moved to follow her out and watched as she set the bowl on the bottom step. She gazed out into the darkness and called out to the cat.

He had no idea if Bluff had run off or if Scott had found her and gotten rid of her to hurt Jane. He blinked hard and peered up into the sky, missing the little ball of fur himself. First light, he'd go out and look around.

"Come back inside," he said.

She turned around, ducked her chin, and walked past him into the kitchen. He hooked her waist. She startled, and he swore. "Sorry, baby. Just need to hold you for a second."

"I'm okay, Kage. Seriously. It's over." She patted his arm.

He let her go, and she walked away from him without looking back. He frowned and followed. It would have made sense for her to be angry, or even to cry. Yet she walked around the house as if she'd arrived home after a day at the garage.

Garrett, Tony, and Lance came in, closing the front door behind them. Jane stopped in the middle of the room and stiffened. Garrett crossed to her and wrapped her in his arms. She held on, head turned, staring at the wall behind Kage. He gritted his teeth. He did not like what he was seeing.

"It's finished, sis," Garrett said.

Jane nodded and pulled back. "Thank you." She gazed at each one of them, but when she looked at Kage, she settled her eyes on the front of his shirt. "To all of you."

Garrett glanced at Kage and back to Jane. "Everything okay?"

"Yeah." She stepped closer. "Can you take me home?"

Garrett's brows rose. "That's what you want?"

"Mm-hmm." She lifted her arm. "I'll just grab a few clothes, and then you can pick up the rest of my things tomorrow."

"Sure, sis," Garrett said, waiting until she walked out of the room before looking at Kage. "Wanna tell me what that's all about?"

"She's in denial." He crossed his arms. "I'll tell you now while she's in the other room, I won't let you walk out the door with her. She's not going anywhere."

Garrett narrowed his eyes. "My sister's life has hung from a very thin thread the last four years, which I've recently found out about and doesn't make me feel good, seeing as how I'm her brother. I watched a drug runner hold a gun on her tonight and, frankly, anything my sister asks me for right now, I'd do in a heartbeat, so tell me one good reason why I would ever leave her with you when it's obvious she doesn't want to be here."

Kage looked him dead in the eye. "Because I love her."

Chapter Twenty-three

The tension that filled Kage's living room could be cut with a knife. Jane walked straight to Garrett, ignoring Kage. Each step she made more painful and desperate for her. She'd brought Scott into Kage's life and put him in the position to stand back while Scott beat her. Her heart broke for the fear and frustration emanating from Kage, and she was responsible for him feeling that way.

He'd survived so much in his life and came back stronger each time, but she feared she finally broke him, and that was the last thing she wanted to do. How would he ever look at her again and still want her? It was one thing for him to hear secondhand about the abuse she'd gone through. It was another to have witnessed how powerless she became around Scott.

He spoke not a word, nor moved toward her, but she could feel his gaze. Each step away from him hurt him in a way she knew he'd never forgive her. She stopped beside Garrett and waited. Her brother lifted his arm, and she shook her head, moving a step away. She'd crack if anyone touched her.

Garrett's brow furrowed, but he respected her wishes. She owed Garrett big-time for what she'd put him through over the last month.

Tired of being the center of everyone's attention, she wanted only to go home. Feeling truly lost without Bluff and now Kage, she walked to the door with her bag hanging from her hand. Away from everything, she could hole up in her bed and pretend that none of this had happened. She'd hold Kage's love inside her heart for the rest of her life and know it was the best thing anyone ever gave her.

"Later." Tony bypassed her and jogged to his Chevy.

"Glad it's done, Janie." Lance winked at her, unsmiling, before heading after Tony.

She stepped off the porch and inhaled deeply, finding it easier to breathe outside.

She listened in the darkness and peered out at the bushes on the edge of the front lawn. "I hope Bluff's o—"

"Baby?" Kage said from behind her.

She stopped and squeezed her eyes closed. Her throat tightened, shutting down her eagerness to respond. The comfort in one endearment tempted her to turn around and fly into his arms.

"Janie, look at me," Kage said.

She opened her eyes and pivoted on her heel. She bit her tongue to keep from sobbing. He gave her the breath to breathe, her strength to be strong, and her will to overcome her past.

"Thought you understood me and what being in my bed meant." He tilted his head. "I promised you I'd never push you out of my life again, and now you're the one walking away. You're killing me, baby."

"Kage…" She glanced at Garrett, who stepped away, giving them space. "I need time."

His pupils constricted, he was that close to her. "Away from me?"

"Yeah," she whispered.

He immediately deflated, and it killed her. "One question…do you love me?" he asked softly.

She pressed her hand to her chest, aching inside. "You know I do."

Kage snapped his gaze up and nodded to Garrett. Her brother stepped in front of her, kissed her cheek gently, and said, "You've haven't been given a choice in a long time, sis. I'm giving you one now. You say the word, and I'll take you home."

She stared up into her brother's eyes and opened her mouth, but the words never came. She grabbed his arm, desperate for him to understand she wanted him. She trusted Kage to tell her if she was doing the right thing. Her decisions always got her in trouble and steered her down the wrong path, but she'd learned to trust herself when it came to him. Her choice to love Kage wasn't wrong or bad.

"I love you." Garrett kissed her forehead and walked away. Behind her, the car door opened and shut. She whipped her head around, scared she was doing more harm than good by staying.

"Let's go inside and talk." Kage slipped his fingers into her hand.

She tugged to free her arm so she could run toward the car to catch Garrett, but Kage pulled her back against him and wrapped both arms around her. With her back tight against him, she watched her brother back out of the yard, not even looking her way.

"I don't want to talk. Let's just savor the moment." She squeezed her eyes shut.

He picked her up on a startled scream and headed toward the house. "Then you can listen, and I'll talk. Every time you want to build a wall around yourself and push me away, you can bet I'll do everything in my power to make you stop."

She kicked out with her legs. "Put me down!"

His arm tightened around her knees. "Not happening."

"Let me go." She hissed through gritted teeth. "I'm through with men who want to boss me around and…and…assholes."

"Good to hear." Kage carried her through the doorway and kicked the door shut. "I'm protective when it comes to my woman. I wouldn't want you around those kinds of men either."

"You're one of them." Jane pushed at his shoulders, and to her relief he put her down. Without missing an opportunity, she scrounged through her bag and found her phone.

"Who are you calling?" he asked.

"Not that it's any of your business, but Sabrina. You're not the only one who has friends who'll have your back. I've got my own friends, and when I need their help, they won't manhandle me and make me do what I don't want to do." She turned on her phone, but Kage ripped it from her hands and threw it against the wall. The cell split in half and the battery ricocheted into the couch.

Jane gasped. "What the hell are you doing?"

"Say it again," he whispered.

She blinked several times without understanding the change in the tone of his voice or his demand. "What?"

"Tell me about your friends."

"I…it doesn't matter." She marched toward the door. "I'll walk all the way home if I have to."

He reached the door first. "You have friends who have your back."

It dawned on her what she said. The implications of what it meant. The knowledge that when she needed her friends, she'd pushed them away. "Don't do this to me."

"Stop hiding."

Jane dropped her gaze. "I can't."

"You can," he said, his voice dropping lower. "You have to, baby. This isn't healthy."

She rounded on him. "You don't think I don't know that? Nothing about me is healthy. I spent four years letting someone beat the crap out of me if I looked at him the wrong way. What kind of person does that? Each time I ran, I'd let myself believe it was the last time…it was finally over and I'd be free. And, every single time, I went back with him. You think the problem is fixed because you captured Scott? It's not, because the problem is in here." She thumped her chest. "*I'm* the problem."

"Janie—"

"It's true." She held her hand in front of her. "Look at what happened between you and me. Three nights, and I'm on my back, you between my legs. That's how desperate I am. You'd already turned me away once, and yet at the first sign of attention from you, I sleep with you. You offered me safety and protection, but you don't really love me."

He frowned. "Why would you say I don't love you?"

"Because you've never told me." Her heart raced, and she gasped for breath. "I can't even think for myself anymore or trust my own judgment. I rely on you for support, because you're strong enough for both of us."

"You're not—"

"One day you'll wake up and realize your good intentions suck, and you're tired of me. I won't do that to you." She sucked in air. "I'll slowly kill whatever we have, and I won't allow another person I care about to die. Do you understand me? I don't want you to die."

He put his hands in his front pockets and his gaze softened. She stood alone, breathing hard, unable to control the way the tightness in her chest splintered, leaving pain throughout her body, robbing her of every thought.

"He died," she said on a sob. "Because of me, Daddy's gone, and I'll never be able to talk with him again or hold his hand. He had huge hands, bigger than anyone I know, and rough. More times than not, he'd leave a spot of grease behind on everything he touched. Do you know how many times I'd glance in a mirror and see a smudge of grease on my chin or cheek because Dad patted my face, just because he loved me?"

"Yes, he loved you," he said.

"He'd always tell me 'I love you, Janie girl.' Then h-he'd pat my head and smile before he cupped my cheek. Always. And, now I'll never feel his touch because his heart couldn't take what I put him through." She cupped her elbows in her hands and curled into herself. "I killed him, and I can't bring him back."

Kage gathered her in his arms, walked to the couch, and sat with her on his lap. She shoved her face into his neck. The guilt of what happened the morning her dad died slowly drowned her. She'd pushed aside her grief in order to survive and nothing, not even Kage, could stop the emptiness inside of her from coming out.

"Your dad had a heart attack, baby," he whispered, stroking her hair.

She shook her head. "He died because I had finally worked up the nerve to call him at three o'clock in the morning after Scott got done teaching me a lesson. I told him everything."

"Jane. That did not kill your dad."

She pushed against Kage and gazed up into his face. "He died outside, beside the car, his keys in his hand, right after I called him to come and get me. All I cared about was someone was finally coming to help me get away from Scott, and instead I killed him."

"Your dad needed a valve replacement, baby. The doctor had been after him for weeks, but he didn't want to take time away from the garage to take care of his health. After he died, the doctor at the hospital told Garrett that his heart simply gave out. It was not because you called and asked for help." Kage held her face between his hands. "He was your father. He could handle the truth. That's his job, and just because it coincided with his heart failing him, you must know that he was doing the one thing he wanted to do. He loved you, and he was coming to help."

"A heart problem?" she said.

He kissed her forehead. "It was not your fault."

She stared at him, not understanding all the new information being thrown at her. Dad had taught her how to be strong and always supported her in whatever she wanted to do. He should've told her about his health problems.

If she'd known, she could've talked with him more. She let out her breath, closed her eyes, and felt Kage swipe moisture across her cheek.

When she opened her eyes, she realized she was crying.

"Let it go," he whispered, pulling her down against his chest. "It's been too damn long. You've never cried. You're too fucking strong."

And maybe, because he gave her his permission, Jane's careful hold on her emotions crumbled. She cried for lost time, for missing her dad's life the last four years, for not being a good sister, and for putting her garbage on Kage's shoulders.

She replayed her life, changing the things she wished could've been different. The happy times and the special moments, no one could take those memories away from her. Most of all, she remembered the boy who always stood up for her, whether it was against her brother or so-called friends she'd lost along the way growing up. She held onto Kage's shirt, afraid he'd let her go.

Hours later, or sometime in the early morning, she woke up in bed, wrapped in Kage's arms. She slid out from under him. Her head was heavy from all the tears, but the pressure in her chest was lighter and less painful.

He propped his head on his hand. "Where are you going?"

"I have to find something." She turned on the bedroom light, squinting against the glare.

She found her shoes at the end of the bed. Wide awake and anxious to show Kage, she smiled at him.

"Is your car locked?" she asked. "I need my purse."

He pushed off the bed. "I'll get it."

"Okay." She pushed her hair out of her face. "I'll start the coffee."

In the kitchen, tears threatened again, and she pushed them away. She rushed to the back door, and opened it. The bowl of cat food still sat full on the step. *Oh, Bluff. Where are you?*

Kage came in the kitchen. "Here's your purse."

"Bluff never came to eat." She closed the door. "Do you think she's okay if she's out there in the woods?"

"Yeah, baby, she's a cat. After being stuck inside the house lately, she's probably exploring. Do you know if she's fixed?" He scratched his chest.

"I-I don't know." She dropped her arms and stared at Kage. "She's was really young and little when I found her. Just a kitten, really."

"I'll take that as a no." He smiled tenderly. "I don't have to explain a female cat's behavior to you, right?"

She fought a grin. "No."

"I checked around the house when I was out there. I didn't find her, but I'll look in the woods and down by the spring before I have to head to work. Are you going to the garage today?"

"Yeah. I want to talk to Garrett," she said.

"Right." Kage sat down at the table and rubbed his hands over his face. "Are we good this morning?"

"Yes." Jane moved in and kissed him. "Thank you. For everything."

He scooped her onto his lap. "More."

She kissed him again.

God. How could she walk away from him, from this? Her lips softened and warmed. His tongued stroked her slow and hot. Pleasure walked up her spine, leaving tingles in its wake. Her belly rolled, turning her insides to mush.

He made everything okay. It felt good, right, exhilarating.

Yet she put her hands on his chest, and pushed him away gently. "I have to show you something."

"Thought that's what you were doing when we were kissing," he said.

"A different something. I was going to show you after the first time we had sex, but you distracted me." She tugged her purse off the table, extracted her wallet, and held it in her lap. "Do you remember when I came home for the funeral?"

"Yeah," he whispered, and his hold on her tightened.

"What you don't know is Scott threatened to make a scene at the funeral if I didn't promise to come back to him." Hatred burned in her stomach at the memory. "I couldn't even concentrate on what was happening at home or with Garrett. I wasn't allowed to mourn Dad the way I wanted. Last night...well, I need to face that he's really gone. I know that."

"There's time. You'll handle it when you're ready, and I'll be right here to help you," he whispered.

"I know," she whispered back. "I knew it that day, and I know it now. What you don't understand is I knew it so long ago that I can't even pinpoint a day when I didn't know that you were something special."

His eyes softened, and she kissed him. "You see, if I look back on the time I lived with Scott, there was one thing that kept me believing that everything was going to be okay. Every time he hit me—"

"Babe. It's over," he said.

"Let me finish, please." She unclipped her wallet and pulled out a piece of paper, handing it to him. "You gave me your phone number the day of the funeral. I held on to it. You can see where the paper's worn and the ink is faded. That's because I held it in my hand whenever I needed to believe I was worth something to someone. The last time I was in the hospital, I kept it wadded up in my fist. I threw a fit if the nurses tried to open my hand. When I went back to the apartment, I put it in my wallet folded and hidden in a receipt so Scott would never find it."

He cleared his throat. "What are you saying?"

"I'm saying…you saved me, Kage. I keep telling myself we're going too fast, that we don't know where this relationship is headed, but I'd be lying if I told you that's how I'm feeling. The truth is I love you. I've loved you since I was seventeen and you refused to kiss me. I know that's not real love, but when I'd dream of the man I wanted, it was always you." She raked her teeth over her bottom lip. "For the last four years, it was you who I thought about and escaped to in my mind when it seemed impossible to go another day living with Scott. When I was in his bed, I pretended I was in yours."

"Fuck," he whispered.

"I'm not going back to keeping my feelings to myself anymore. I've hurt too many people by living a lie." Jane stroked his jaw. "I know you don't feel the same way, and I'm okay with that. But I'm not leaving your bed again. It's where I always wanted to be."

"Say it again," he said.

"What?"

"The truth." His jaw ticked as he fought a grin. "I need to hear you tell me."

"I love you," she whispered against his lips.

He kissed her hard, possessive, demanding. Her need to show him what she was feeling was pushed to the side as he took everything from her, stripping her of the worry over spilling her secrets. He accepted and gave back tenfold.

Both of them panting, he pulled back softly, giving her small kisses, until he laid his forehead against hers. "Love you too, baby. Always have. Just had to wait. I'm done waiting."

She melted. "I get you."

Chapter Twenty-four

Kage slid under the black Corvair convertible on a dolly. Garrett handed him the air wrench, while Lance and Tony held the new chrome bumper onto the frame. Jane elbowed Sabrina, grinning at the men. Both of them sat on the tool bench in front of the car, content to watch the guys from Body Shop do their magic.

"I told Kage I loved him yesterday," Jane said.

Sabrina swayed sideways with the radio playing, twirling a welding rod. "I heard about it already."

She tilted her head. "From who?"

"Kage. I overheard him talking to Garrett in the john." Sabrina grinned and tossed the rod beside her on the bench. "You should've seen Garrett go all big brother on him. It was hilarious. I thought Kage was going to punch him."

"He didn't tell me." She sighed. It figured Kage would confide in Garrett, they were best friends, but Garrett was her brother, and she wanted to make up for lost time by spreading all the good news around. "Hey, what were you doing in the bathroom with them?"

"You've seen the one they built in the agency. It's sweet. No way am I going to use the garage bathroom. It's not fit for a woman." Sabrina hopped down off the bench.

"Wait." She jumped to the floor. "How often do you hang out here?"

Sabrina smiled and walked away, leaving Jane more confused than ever. Why would Sabrina come to the garage so often when Jane was working and not stop into the office to say hi?

"That's it." Kage handed out the air tool and rolled out from under the car. "This one's done."

Garrett and Lance walked back ten feet, studying the Corvair and grinning appreciatively. Sabrina pushed her way between Garrett and Lance, joining them in their admiration. Jane hung back, warmed by the scene. She'd witnessed the moment of completion on many a job. Even before Garrett and the guys had taken over the shop she'd often watched her dad rolling a car out to the customer. There was something about the pride and male satisfaction that comforted her.

"Hey, baby." Kage walked toward her. "Want to hand me that rag?"

She reached behind her, picked up the old used T-shirt, and tossed it to him. He wiped the grease from his hands, leaned in, and kissed her.

"What're you thinking?" he asked.

"Does Sabrina come here a lot? I mean, before I came home."

He chuckled and shrugged. "I guess so. Why?"

"Don't you think it's strange? Not that she's not welcome here, but hello…it's just a bunch of guys working." She unzipped his coveralls and slid her hands inside and around his waist.

He stood still, letting her get her feel of him without getting her greasy. "Sabrina's got a thing for Garrett."

"A thing? Like…a thing, thing?" She stepped away.

Kage grinned. "Yeah, although your brother's ignoring her."

"Why?"

"Don't know." He peeled his arms out of the coveralls, pulled a stool closer, and sat. "That's his business."

"Not anymore." She stepped forward.

Kage tagged her waist and hauled her onto his lap. "Stay out of it."

"But he's my brother and she's my best friend." She bounced on his legs. "This is freaking fantastic!"

He tilted her back. She squealed, wrapping her arms around his neck. These moments, Kage carefree and playful, she wouldn't give up for anything.

After sharing all her bottled-up feelings with Kage the last two days, she looked forward to whatever came next between them. She spent her days at the garage. Most of the time that meant spending it with Kage, unless he went out on a case for a few hours. At night, she slept in his bed.

"Knock it off, you two." Garrett flicked her hair over her face. "I have a truck full of your shit I was going to haul to Kage's for you, but we're all going to the bar for a drink first. Lance is buying."

"The hell I am. Last time I offered, I ended up buying everyone's dinner too." Lance unzipped the leg on his coveralls. "It's Janie's turn."

She grinned at the use of her nickname. "Fine. I'll buy."

Kage nuzzled her neck. "I'll buy."

"I got it covered." She squirmed when he licked her under the ear. "I'm loaded."

He stiffened.

She sat straighter, dropping her arms. "What?"

"Meeting. Now," he announced to everyone, standing her up.

He walked over to the wall, pushed the buttons for all three bay doors to close, and whistled loudly to gain everyone's attention. Sabrina walked toward Jane, and she shrugged at the questioning look.

Kage returned to the group. "Jane's still got the money."

"Shit. How did we forget about that?" Tony ran both hands through his hair.

Lance shook his head, leaned against the bench, and crossed his boots. "We let ourselves lose our heads. She's one of our own."

Warmth flooded her. She was back in, and they claimed her.

"If we turn the money in that implicates Jane more, even though I don't think it'll matter when it comes time for the trial. They have enough on Carson to send him away," Garrett said.

Kage shook his head. "The money isn't Carson's, though. We know who the money belongs to. Darrell won't let her walk off free to spend what is his. You turn it in, and he'll still come after Jane. He won't want the shields involved."

"What do you suggest?" Tony brushed his hair off his forehead. "You're not thinking of walking in and handing it back to your uncle. That's suicide, man."

"No one is asking me, and I won't let Kage have the money. He's no longer involved." Jane wrapped her arm around Kage's waist. He raised his brows. She shook her head, stopping him from talking. "I'll mail it to him."

Lance laughed, then quickly stopped when Kage shot him a look, but his lips quivered as he tried not to grin. "Bro, it's not a bad idea."

"And look like a puss?" Kage put his arm around her. "I'll deal with the money and Darrell tomorrow. It's too late now to make any decisions. I need a beer. Let's go to Corner Pocket."

After locking up the office and the front door, Jane headed down the hallway—pausing to shut Kage's locker—and joined the boys at the back door, along with Sabrina. She leaned into Kage.

She waited for the others to walk out. "Can I ask you something?" she asked him.

He leaned against the wall and pulled her with him until she pressed along the length of him. "Yeah."

"What's with the photo in your locker? A street?"

He dropped his chin before looking her square in the eyes. "A reminder to always walk on the right side. I took it with the camera the Dentons gave me when I first moved in with them after my dad went to prison. Kept it, because it reminds me of where I could be and where I want to be."

Oh, wow. She braced her hand on his stomach, stretched to her toes, and kissed him. "You have more integrity than anyone I know. I've always loved that about you."

His eyes grew soft, and he relaxed. "And I'm going to keep walking the right way, baby. I won't ever forget. I got you now. Got everything I want."

Garrett opened the door, stuck his head inside, and raised his brows. "Coming?"

Kage hooked his finger in the loop of her jeans and kept her from walking out. "Yeah, give us a sec."

Her brother let the door close, and when they were alone, Kage said, "I'm paying."

"It's not a big deal. I do have money from Garrett I get for working for him. I won't touch dirty money." She patted his chest and kissed him. "Besides, it makes me feel good to be part of the group again. I missed this, and I owe them a lot."

"You don't get it. I'm paying." He stood straighter, so she couldn't kiss him again.

"Does this have to do with the whole subject of me in your bed, ugh, 'you're my woman, let me drag you to my house by your hair' thing you got going on?" she asked.

His cheek twitched and he laughed. Not in a ha-ha-that's-funny but in a you're-freaking-hilarious kind of way that made her happy to let him get away with his caveman act. "Yeah, baby, that's it."

She smiled. "Okay then. You're paying."

"Yeah?"

She shrugged. "It's sexy the way you want to take care of me. Gives me butterflies in a good way."

"Fuck," he murmured. "Butterflies?"

"Yeah." She opened the doors. "It's like foreplay with my clothes on."

His laughter followed her around the corner of the building and then came to a complete stop. She turned, surprised to see his face go hard, even scary.

She moved toward him. "Kage?"

A tall, good-looking man stood next to a black Lexus. The cut of his suit fit his frame to a T. She studied his face, unable to hide her shock. "Shit. He looks just like you…"

He stepped between her and the man.

"Is that Darrell Archer? Your uncle?" She peered around Kage. "Oh, sweet baby Jesus. He's coming toward us."

Kage's hand settled on her hip, and he pushed her behind him. She slipped her fingers under his belt. Afraid his uncle would demand that Kage go away with him, she planned to keep him here, safe and with her.

"Kage." Darrell stopped ten feet in front of them. "I believe your woman has something that doesn't belong to her."

"I'm aware of that." Kage's fingers tightened on her hip. "I don't appreciate you showing up here, and I especially don't like how you feel free to contact me when my woman is with me."

"I'm sure you understand that it would be better if she handed over what she stole, so I can be on my way." Darrell shrugged, and the motion reminded her so much of Kage. And yet the scumbag wasn't even good enough to look at him, let alone talk to him. "Considering you used your only marker, it's in your best interest if we don't have this unfortunate misunderstanding between us."

"Kage," she whispered.

He tapped her side but continued speaking to Darrell. "I'll meet you tomorrow. Name the place."

She rolled her eyes. "Kage?"

"Not now, baby." Kage widened his stance.

"I believe your woman wants to say something," Darrell said.

"Finally," she muttered, stumbling out from behind Kage and straightening her shirt. "Mr. Archer?"

"Fuck." Kage growled and tried to grab her wrist.

She shook him off and gave him a pointed look before turning her attention to his uncle. "I have your money right here in my purse."

"Jesus. You're carrying it all on you?" Kage cussed under his breath.

"I have to do this," she whispered. "Remember, we talked about closure. Now I can be done with Scott Carson and your uncle will leave you alone."

She pulled out the wad of cash she had wrapped with a rubber band. Kage snagged it out of her hand and pointed at the ground. "Stay put. Do not move, or so help me…"

She shivered but could not hide the grin on her face. He shook his head, and it sure seemed like he was reading her mind because his cheek twitched. Her man was hot.

Kage marched the remaining feet separating him from his uncle. After handing the money to Darrell, he pivoted and walked straight back to her. She smiled. It was finally over.

"Kage," Darrell called.

Kage turned. "We're done. Any business that brought us back into each other's space is over. I expect you to respect the lines."

Darrell nodded. "You're still my nephew. My blood flows in your veins."

Kage remained silent. Jane slipped her hand into his, and he squeezed. He rarely talked about the turmoil of being an Archer, but she trusted Kage, she loved him, and she would support him in his quest to walk on the right side of the road.

"I have something for your woman." Darrell smiled at Jane. "A welcome-to-the-family gift, if nothing else."

"Not happening." Kage extracted his hand from Jane's and looped his arm across her shoulders.

Darrell lifted his arm and motioned toward the car. The back door opened and a beautiful woman in a sexy black skirt and deep blue shirt climbed out. Kage stiffened. Jane looked at Kage and back to the woman.

She was stunning with black wavy hair, a dusky complexion with almost an exotic slant to her eyes. Jane stepped closer to Kage, unsure what this woman meant to him.

Kage's grip tightened even more. The woman held her arms crossed in front of her as she walked toward them. She spotted the gray fur peeking out of the nook of the lady's arm.

"Bluff," she whispered, swaying against Kage.

The woman approached her and held out the cat. "She's a very nice cat, and I do believe she belongs to you."

Jane nodded her head, accepting the gift and holding Bluff tight to her chest. Unsure what to say, she stood silently, blinking through the tears clouding her vision. The woman dropped her gaze and returned to the car. Darrell lifted his chin to Kage and headed back to the Lexus.

Kage wrapped his arm around her back and pulled her tight to his side. They stayed together until the Lexus drove away. She rained kisses on the sweet spot between Bluff's ears. *You're safe, Bluff. We have Kage now.*

Chapter Twenty-five

The rowdy atmosphere inside Corner Pocket fit Jane's mood. The drinks came fast, the music played even faster, and all her friends crowded around, admiring Bluff. She leaned to the side and kissed Charlene's cheek.

"Thanks, hon. I couldn't bear to leave her alone in the car when I thought I might have lost her forever." She passed the cat to Sabrina.

"If the inspector comes while you're here, slip out the back door. Understand?" Charlene winked.

"Perfectly." Jane smiled. "Nobody will know we were even here."

Across the table, Sabrina sat down beside Garrett. She couldn't help staring. The thought of those two getting together thrilled her. If only her brother would wise up and see that Sabrina was crushing on him. So far, he hadn't clued in on what everyone else saw when they were together.

Garrett lifted his beer, eyeing the cat, and fell into watching Sabrina with Bluff. Jane squeezed Kage's thigh under the table. Her brother could deny his attraction to Sabrina all he wanted, but he was definitely noticing her. He couldn't keep his eyes off her whenever she wasn't looking at him, which was almost constantly.

She leaned against Kage's arm. "How do you think your uncle got a hold of Bluff?"

"Don't know and probably won't find out." Kage leaned back and put his arm across the back of the booth. "If you're ever alone and he approaches you, I want you to walk away. No acting tough. He's not a man to trust."

"Do you think he'll bother you again?"

His fingers went to the back of her head, pulling her closer to him. "Yeah. There's no running away from family, despite my hate for him. He's bad news, baby. We can't ever let our guard down."

She nodded. She understood his worry, but he wasn't alone anymore.

Tony strolled to the table and squatted down on Jane's side but looked at Kage. "Hey, that woman who was with your uncle at the garage…you know her?"

Kage shook his head. "Nope. She's probably one of his women, unless he's changed his ruling and is bringing females underground."

"Damn." Tony inhaled through his nose. "I could swear I've met her before, but that's crazy."

Kage leaned forward. "Why?"

"There was a woman, down in Clatsop County, going through the police academy a year ago when I took a safety course for my concealed weapons permit. She was doing drills outside with her squad when we broke for lunch. Smoking hot, you'd never imagine she'd lift a hand and risk breaking a nail, but she was tough. She looks exactly like the woman with Archer." Tony stood. "Damn, she was sexy. Just thinking about her, you knew she'd burn you."

Kage stiffened. "You think this woman is the same one and will cause problems for the police bureau?"

"Nah, I doubt if it was her. Probably a good thing, since Archer has a habit of ruining any woman connected with him. Besides, I can't see him getting cozy with a shield." Tony heaved a sigh.

"Tony! Get your ass over here." Lance motioned from the pool table. "Hurry up and break, I have to leave in fifteen minutes for a two-day stakeout."

Tony walked off, and Jane curled into Kage. "Let's go home. I've had enough excitement for the day."

He kissed her forehead. "You got it."

She stood beside the table, hugged Garrett goodbye, and pried Bluff out of Sabrina's arms. Warmth flooded her at having her cat back with her.

"You need to go to the little kitty's room? Hm?" She rubbed her nose on Bluff's ears before turning to Garrett and Sabrina. "Thanks for everything, you guys. I swear, from here on out, I won't cause any trouble."

"Stop thanking us." Sabrina gave her a one-armed hug. "We'll talk tomorrow. Maybe I'll stop in at the garage and we can make plans to hit the mall this weekend if you can get away from Kage long enough."

"You're not hanging out at the garage. We have work to do." Garrett crossed his arms. "It's not a place for women."

Sabrina only smiled. "Like I said, I'll come by the garage."

"Sounds like a plan." Jane fought a grin.

Kage curled his arm around her neck and led her toward the door. Before they reached the exit, Charlene planted herself in their path. With her fists on her hips, she stared up at Kage.

"I don't have that much time, and I've decided I'm not letting this go without saying something." She hitched her thumb at Jane. "The girl loves you."

Kage raised his brow. "Good thing, since she's sleeping in my bed."

Charlene shook her head. "I mean, she loves you, not loves sleeping with you."

"I know that too," Kage's murmured.

"Oh." Charlene looked at Jane. "You've had a lot on your mind lately, and a little slow to catch on. Do I have to explain what he's doing with you, because he might've had more women than we can count, but he's never taken one to his house and especially not his best friend's sister."

Jane laughed, glancing up into Kage's eyes. "I think I get it."

Charlene studied them both. They grinned back.

"Come here and give me some lovin' too, and then get your butts home." Charlene held out her arms. "You two are going to make me cry. I'm hap-skippy for you."

"Thanks, Charlene," Jane whispered, holding her friend. "It means a lot to both of us."

On the car ride home, Jane stroked Bluff's back as the cat slept on her lap. She replayed the day, and couldn't deny that Kage's uncle freaked her out a little bit.

From all the stories she'd heard, she'd been expecting a monster, but he looked so much like Kage, it surprised her.

"Can I ask you something?" She turned to him.

"Yeah."

"There must've been a time in your life when it would've been easier to stay with your uncle after your father went away. What made you decide to step away from your family?" she asked.

"You," he said.

"No. I'm serious." She leaned her head back against the seat. "You were just a boy, and family means security to a child. You'd just lost your mom and dad."

He pulled onto the lane heading toward his house and slowed down on the gravel road. "I am serious. There was a time, I did think about going with Uncle Darrell. I was struggling with building a good reputation for myself, but it wasn't easy. The Dentons tried to talk with me, but I was young and headstrong, then later the hormones hit and every day seemed like a struggle. I guess I was afraid to rely on them. Looking back, I should've."

"So, they set a good example for you?"

"Yeah. They were pillars of the community, and demanded respect. That kind of presence got attention from everyone they met." He turned into the driveway and cut the engine. "That's not what motivated me though. Like I said, it was you."

"I don't understand. We were friends through my brother, but I was younger than you." She slipped her seat belt off without waking Bluff.

"You're not the only one who wanted to kiss the night you woke me up on the couch, baby." His gaze warmed and he sighed, his lips curving. "You were beautiful. I swore from that day on, I wouldn't do anything to make you doubt what kind of a man I was. I wanted you to look at me and see Kage, not another Archer. Then I waited, hoping one day we'd run into each other, the timing would be right, and you would see I'm nothing like my family."

Oh, wow. She swallowed. "I didn't know..."

He smiled and cupped her cheek. "Now you do, so what are you going to do with the information?"

She laughed softly. "Take you to bed?"

"Good answer."

Inside the front door, he took Bluff from her, set the cat on the floor, and kissed Jane. She wrapped her arms around his neck, her legs around his hips, and took everything he offered with his mouth.

When his lips left hers and trailed along her neck, she whispered, "I want you."

"Fuck," he muttered, holding her tighter. The evidence of how much he wanted her was evident in the hardness of his body.

He carried her to the bed, set her on the mattress, and planted his hands on either side of her. She squirmed out of her jeans, taking her panties off too. Then she wiggled out of her shirt, melting as he stripped out of his own clothes. "I need you right now."

"Don't want to be anywhere else." He slipped the laces out of his black boots, kicked them off, and toed off his socks.

She managed to smile through the tears pooling in her vision. "I love you."

"I love you too, baby," he whispered back.

He ran his cheek against hers, his whiskers tickling her skin. She shivered at the tenderness he gave her. His hand roamed up her belly to her breast.

"I never want a time when you're not in bed with me." His voice filled with emotion sent her stomach fluttering.

"'Kay," she agreed, because sleeping without him wasn't possible. He made her feel safe, loved, and most of all, she wanted to give him something he needed.

Then his hand slid between her legs, and his long finger filled her. His mouth latched onto her nipple. She arched off the mattress at the deep pull that shot straight to her core. She sank her fingers into his hair and moaned.

He slid out of her, circling, stroking, and bringing her higher. Emotionally raw and vulnerable, everything hit her at once, and she spiraled out of control. So desperate to connect with him, she could feel her orgasm building before he even entered her.

He removed his mouth and his hand and she whimpered.

"Together, baby. Don't come without me. Not tonight. I need you," he said.

He grabbed behind her knees and pulled her legs up, spreading her more. She latched her ankles around his waist. His weight came down. He slid into her, so hard, so heavy, and so pleasurable. Her back came off the bed again. "Kage."

He moved back and forth. Fast and hard. She reached up and wrapped her hands around the back of his neck, lifting her upper body, and kissed him. Her tongue clashed with his, and he ground his pelvis against her with each stroke of his hardness.

He sped up, taking and giving, needing her as much as she needed him. She scrambled to get closer, almost frantic in her need to ease the hurt that had touched both their lives. He growled in her mouth, and the vibration was enough to push her over the edge. Every cell in her body exploded, and she hung on to him, loving every deep pulse in her lower stomach.

He tore his mouth away from hers and threw his head back, groaning his release.

She came down from the orgasm gently with the help of soft, long strokes from Kage. She collapsed on the bed, smiling lazily up at him. She roamed her hands across his chest, amazed at the strength coming from one man.

And he was her man. Stubborn, strong, and honorable with a touch of badass. She smiled tenderly. He was perfect for her.

"I always want to see a smile on your face, baby." He rolled off her, bringing her with him.

The seriousness of what they were creating together excited her. "Honey, I do love you. I don't want you to think I said it just to say it."

He ran his finger along the curve of her cheek. "I know."

She caught his hand. "I'm sorry. I screwed up everything we could've had together. I just never imagined—"

"It's over. Done." He shushed her. "We're together now."

They lay in each other's arms, catching their breath. Bluff jumped onto the bed and rubbed against Kage before climbing onto his chest and settling down. She smiled. Her badass guy and her cat. Watching them together was about the most adorable thing she'd ever seen, but she kept that thought to herself.

"Take your cat, baby. I need to get something." He waited until she settled Bluff on the mattress beside her before getting off the bed and walking out of the room.

"What do you think he's doing, kitty? Maybe he's going to feed you, hmm?" She stifled a yawn. "It's good to have you home, Bluff."

Kage walked back into the bedroom carrying a bag. She sat up, reaching for her shirt, and slipped it over her head. He leaned down and kissed her.

He handed her the sack. "It's for you."

"What is it?" She held the gift and smiled at him.

"Something you need." He sat beside her.

She scrambled to her knees. "A gun?"

"No gun." He groaned, hooking her neck and chuckling into her ear. "Something more important."

She opened the drawstring and peeked inside. A box lay at the bottom. She flashed her gaze at him. Oh. My. God.

She dove inside and pulled out a red velvet hinged box. She paused, looking at him. "Seriously?"

H tilted his brow. "Open it, baby."

Inside, a gold ring with two diamonds, side by side, sparkled up at her. Kage took the ring out of the box and slipped it onto the finger of her left hand. She struggled for breath.

"What's this mean?" she whispered.

"I know you're in my bed. You know you're in my bed." He brought her hand up to his lips and kissed her fingers. "Now everyone will know you belong to me."

She blinked through the tears. "This is way better than a gun."

He tossed the bag out of his way, lay her down on the bed, and hovered above her. "I love you, baby."

"I love you too."

Then he kissed her. Again. And again.

Look for the next sexy, suspenseful
Hard Body Novel!

See the next page for a preview of
Weston.

Chapter One

In an abandoned warehouse on Merchant Avenue, the warm stench of fear tickled Rocki's nose. She clamped her teeth to keep from gagging. She'd witnessed enough questionable dealings in the last four months of working undercover, trying to get the goods on Darrell Archer, but nothing prepared for this senseless beating.

Despite her revulsion of how business in the underground took place, hope soared inside her. Finally, Archer trusted her enough to let her hang around while he took care of business. This was exactly what she needed, because so far, she had nothing concrete to bring him down and put him in prison for life.

Darrell's team, comprised of four men, bigger and more evil than she could've ever imagined, dragged an unconscious man she only knew as Joe toward the exit. Joe, who hadn't paid his debt and foolishly thought he could outrun the underground drug lord.

"Come, Camilla." Darrell crooked his finger and walked past her toward the front of the building.

Going by her fake name, she followed him out of the building. Doing what he asked, when he asked, allowed her to stick beside him in her attempt to gather evidence. She wanted him locked in prison for a long, long, long time. The problem was, the information she'd collected wasn't enough to take him down, and she couldn't escape and go back to her normal job of working cases until he went away for good.

In the backseat of Archer's black Lexus, she buckled her seat belt, crossed her legs, and stared straight ahead. As his personal assistant, there were certain things he required of her.

Companionship she could do. A specific job she might do, depending on if it involved blood or not. Today proved she wasn't up to witnessing a few hard punches to someone's face. The seriousness of the situation made it hard to keep believing poor Joe only suffered a broken nose. She had no idea what would happen to him out of her line of sight.

Sex she definitely wouldn't do. Archer had no reason to know that yet. He seemed to enjoy touching her hands, her arms, and giving her an occasional pat on the ass to get her moving out of the room when business was going down. She played it cool, and so far, he retreated when she became uncomfortable. Whether he understood her reluctance and disgust, or he simply wasn't interested, was anyone's guess.

Archer, even at fifty-three years old, kept a steady stream of women coming and going in his life. She swallowed her shiver. Not all of them ran errands for him, unless you counted running to his bed whenever he snapped his fingers a chore. She suspected any woman who displeased him ended up on a ship out of the country and sold into the sex slave business, but she hadn't gathered any proof. She just had a bad feeling.

Most of the women she'd seen were more than happy to hang around him. The black hair with a sprinkle of silver peppered at his temples and the controlling attitude was a total turn-on for some women. Not her though.

She'd give up the job, go into hiding, and start over somewhere else before she allowed herself to go there with him. She wasn't blind. There was something mysteriously charismatic about Archer. And something equally dangerous. Those qualities made him unpredictable.

Darrell eyed her in the rearview mirror. "I have an assignment for you. In a few minutes, I'll be dropping you off near the corner of Main and Elm Street. There will be a red convertible Porsche with keys under the mat."

She blinked, keeping quiet. He'd tell her more or not, depending on how much he wanted her to know. The last time she interrupted, he'd locked her in the house for two days and forbidden her to join him on business.

"The GPS is programmed. Follow the directions straight to your destination. A place called Corner Pocket. When you get there, you'll take possession of the third pool table in the back. I want you to stay at the table all evening." He turned onto a side road. "You'll pay attention to the men who will challenge you to a game. Drink, get loose, and report back to me tomorrow at noon."

"Noon?" She clamped her lips together, shocked she'd lost her cool.

That meant she'd have to find lodgings, but at least she'd have a chance to call her mom without the fear of being overheard. She gazed out the window to appear aloof to the plans. Four months, and Darrell hadn't trusted her away from his side. She slept in a spare bedroom, and when she wasn't with him, he kept her locked in the house and under surveillance.

"At least one of the men will spend the evening vying for your attention. You'll be receptive to his attentions and go home with him. You're to keep your ears open and bring back all information you learn, no matter how mundane you believe it is." Darrell pulled to the curb and left the engine idling. "I don't have to remind you not to mention your association with me or your true identity. You're a stranger traveling through town."

"Of course," she murmured, holding his gaze in the mirror.

"The car is across the road and down one block. Don't disappoint me…"

She nodded and opened the door. She knew her job, and hell to the no, she didn't want to end up like poor Joe back at the warehouse who was probably resting in peace with the fish in the Pacific Ocean by now.

Archer took off the moment the door shut. She stood on the sidewalk, getting her bearings. The area was familiar.

Bay City, Oregon, a half hour away from the police academy where she'd trained, worked on the force, and taught classes while working her way up the ladder. The youngest and only female on the squad, she expected the Archer case to take her to top detective when her supervisor, Detective Gino Marcelli, retired. Unless the special undercover job took longer and she failed to bring in Archer. Or Archer killed her. God, she hoped not.

The streetlights flickered on, and she realized how long they'd dealt with business at the warehouse. They'd left Archer's house before lunch. She crossed the two-lane street, anxious to start playing her role for the night. At least in a public place, she'd have the ability to make a call home. She missed her mom terribly.

The Porsche sat unlocked, top down, and looking sweeter than any ride she'd driven. She trailed her finger along the sleek side of the car, stopping at the door handle. Sliding into the tan leather driver's seat, she exhaled on a sigh. This sure beat her two-thousand-dollar used Honda Accord sitting in her garage.

Her chest tightened as she found the key, started the car, and put her seat belt on. She blinked away the pang of loneliness threatening to overcome her. For the first time since becoming Camilla Darrow, she wanted to leave the dirtiness behind and be herself.

Rocki Bangli.

Tonight, she'd go by Rocki and enjoy answering to her own name. No one needed to know any more details about her. She couldn't take the chance of someone recognizing the odd-sounding last name and asking around about her.

Five minutes later, she strolled into Corner Pocket. A quaint bar on the edge of town, half sports bar and half hangout, displaying the cheesiest neon lighted sign behind the bar with a sexily clad mannequin straddling the letter C. She grinned and relaxed. The place was tacky and homey enough; she loved the bar instantly.

Whether the adrenaline of having time to herself away from Archer or the scent of greasy fries and cold beer brought out the fact she hadn't eaten since morning, she looked forward to tonight. She walked to the counter and slid onto a stool.

An older woman, hair teased out at least six inches on all sides and wearing a vibrant purple spandex yoga jacket lined with faux diamonds down the sleeve and making a wide swoop across the front, displaying a lot of cleavage, approached her. "I'm Charlene, hon. What can I get you?"

She looked inside her purse, unprepared, and blew out her breath at seeing what Archer left her. He'd loaded her with money. "A burger, everything but onions, large fries, and a beer…lite."

An older man leaned over the counter, kissed Charlene's cheek, and whispered in her ear. Rocki took in the intimate scene.

The booming laughter coming from a woman who was no bigger than five feet five inches surprised her. She glanced behind her, searching for her destination. Table 3 was vacant, and she turned back around. "Are there any rules on reserving one of the pool tables?"

"Nope." Charlene stuck the pen she'd used for writing the order in her hair. "If you play the game, you're responsible for the results."

"Ah, gotcha," she said. "I'll grab a table in the back."

"I'll bring your order out when it's up." Charlene paused. "Are you here alone, hon?"

She nodded.

Charlene grinned, shaking her head in amusement. "I'll bet ten dollars that you won't be alone for long. You girls nowadays, I don't know why you force yourself to be so independent. A good man by your side is a life perk."

She slid off the stool and watched Charlene walk away. Any other day, she would've loved to sit down and strike up a conversation with the flamboyant woman. She bet Charlene was a kick, just her type of friend.

Remembering what she came for, she pivoted and headed toward the rear of the room. The third pool table remained empty, and she wondered how Archer knew it would be. Knowing him, he'd paid to have the table cleared and waiting for her.

With no idea who the men were that would show up, or if they'd approach her, she picked out a cue stick from the stand on the wall. She'd played pool exactly twice before.

One time at her friend Gigi's house when she was a sophomore in high school, she learned a few things about the game of pool. She totally sucked but had fun. Then she played it again at Cale Brown's retirement party from the sheriff's department. She sucked then too.

She rounded up all the balls and set them at the end of the table. She knew the basic rules. You hit the white ball into other balls, not letting it go in a hole. You called solids or stripes and tried to beat your opponent by sinking all your balls in the corner and side pockets. On the player's last turn, you hit the black ball, winning the game.

Basically, she knew enough to bluff her way through a game. Her stomach flip-flopped. She'd ignored the fact that the men she'd spend time with tonight were connected to Archer somehow. She hoped they were innocent hits, and her safety wasn't at risk. If they were business associates, she could be in more danger than she already was.

A shrill scream penetrated the bar. She whirled, afraid a fight had broken out. Away from Archer, she'd have to rely on herself for protection. Anyone witnessing the precise movements of the way she fought would know she'd spent years training in physical combat.

Instead of danger, she watched a group of men stroll into the bar. Charlene hurried around the counter, heading straight toward them. Rocki leaned her hip against the table, struck by the jaw-dropping beautiful scene. The men were hot.

Three males, all different in looks but gorgeous just the same. The one leading the pack, dressed in all black with the coolest goatee trimmed close to his skin, yet dark and prominent, smiled. Her brows rose before she could stop herself. He knew the affect he had on women, she was sure of it.

The next guy to approach Charlene had warm brown hair, almost ginger in color, but not quite. He held his arms out wide and laughed heartily when Charlene smacked him on the chest and pushed him out of the way. She peered closer, wondering what grabbed Charlene's attention, and spotted a woman tucked against the side of one of the men. Of course, she'd be beautiful to have a man equally gorgeous.

Dressed in jeans, suede boots, and a purple T-shirt with the words *Jacked* on the front, the woman left the man's side to allow Charlene to wrap her in a hug. The two women's mutual delight in seeing one another spoke of a close relationship, and their reactions fascinated her. She scraped her teeth over her bottom lip.

She didn't know these people. Yet she envied what they had. The normalcy of their lives.

Four long months of working undercover, without any contact with the real world, were apparently getting to her. She gazed away to check out the rest of the group.

Another man, more sexy than the others with a badass attitude, strode through the door and stopped behind them. His expression warmed as he surveyed the people in front of him. He slapped the woman's gorgeous man on the shoulder, spoke to him, and then headed across the room. Aware of her staring, she turned around and fiddled with the racked balls on the table. The last thing she needed to do was become distracted by a handsome face.

And the guy had it all.

Longish blond hair of multiple shades and tanned skin, as if he spent a lot of time outside, gave him a toughness that belied his golden good looks. She couldn't help noticing the tight fit of his leather jacket, black Metallica T-shirt, and jeans—if she guessed right—that had rubbed up against a few car engines in their lifetime. She always had a weakness for men who worked with their hands and weren't afraid to get dirty.

She lifted the triangle thingy, eyed the balls, and deemed the setup perfect. She stepped away from the table to set the rack back on the hanger and bumped into the man who'd grabbed her attention. The blond one. The tough one. The one who appeared a lot scarier up close than she would've suspected. The intense way he looked at her didn't help set her at ease.

"Sorry," she muttered, backing away.

His eyes softened. "You set the balls wrong."

"Excuse me?" she said.

"You need to rack them so the solids and stripes are beside each other and put them behind this line." He slipped the triangle out of her hand. "Let me show you."

"Uh…okay." She gripped the pool stick with both hands and held on for dear life.

She had to get rid of him. At any moment, she expected her targets to show up and challenge her to a game of pool. She glanced down at the man's boots and held her breath. Could these be the men Archer had sent her to find? No, not this guy. He had too much sexy going on.

"Jumping the gun, bro." A male voice spoke behind her.

She looked over her shoulder and stepped a few feet away.

The three other men who'd come in and the woman with them stood at the table taking an interest. Her gaze returned to the blond guy. *No way. No fricking way.*

"Just setting them up for the lady. Looks like we're out of luck tonight. She beat us to the table." The man winked at her. "Name's Tony Weston. Yours?"

"Rocki Ba…just Rocki." She shuffled closer to Tony. Shocked to discover these were the men Archer wanted her to investigate and afraid she wasn't up to the job. "You all can play, if you want. I don't mind."

"Right," he murmured. "We could make this interesting in exchange for sharing the table."

"Oh, yeah?" She inhaled swiftly, wondering if he was in on the meeting and testing her. "What do you have in mind?"

Tony's grin turned into a genuine smile, and the effect wasn't lost on her. She felt the warmth all over, and she meant every little out-of-the-way, hidden spot on her body went suddenly hot. "One game. Winner calls."

"Calls anything?" She gulped.

He leaned in closer and whispered, "Anything."

About the Author

Romance author Debra Kayn lives with her family in the beautiful coastal mountains of Oregon on a hobby farm. She enjoys riding motorcycles, gardening, playing tennis, and fishing. A huge animal lover, she always has a dog under her desk when she writes and chickens standing at the front door looking for a treat. She's famous in her family for teaching a 270-pound hog named Harley to jog with her every morning.

Her love of family ties and laughter makes her a natural to write heartwarming contemporary stories to the delight of her readers. Oh, let's cut to the chase. She loves to write about real men and the women who love them.

When Debra was nineteen years old, a man kissed her without introducing himself. When they finally came up for air, the first words out of his mouth were *Will you have my babies?* Considering Debra's weakness for a sexy, badass man who is strong enough to survive her attitude, she said yes. A quick wedding at the House of Amour and four babies later, she's living her own romance book.